If he had one shred of decency he would let her go

He would send her back to where she'd come from, no better or worse than when she'd left. Back to her fiancé, and her steady, boring existence.

But he knew he wouldn't do it. She was sensitive, and naive—and incredibly innocent—and he was about to ruin her life. But she made him feel alive again.

He frowned, amazed at how proprietary he felt toward her. She belonged to him, he thought irrationally—not to her fiancé. *He'd* decide when he'd let her go. And it might not be as soon as he'd thought.

ANNE MATHER began her career by writing the kind of book she likes to read—romance. Married, with two children, this author from the north of England has become a favorite with readers of romance fiction the world over—her books have been translated into many languages and are read in countless countries. Since her first novel was published in 1970, Anne Mather has written more than eighty romances, with over ninety million copies sold!

Books by Anne Mather

STORMSPELL
WILD CONCERTO
HIDDEN IN THE FLAME
THE LONGEST PLEASURE

HARLEQUIN PRESENTS

1444—BLIND PASSION
1458—SUCH SWEET POISON
1492—BETRAYED
1514—DIAMOND FIRE
1542—GUILTY
1553—DANGEROUS SANCTUARY

HARLEQUIN ROMANCE

1631—MASQUERADE
1656—AUTUMN OF THE WITCH

Anne Mather

Rich As Sin

Harlequin Books

TORONTO • NEW YORK • LONDON
AMSTERDAM • PARIS • SYDNEY • HAMBURG
STOCKHOLM • ATHENS • TOKYO • MILAN
MADRID • WARSAW • BUDAPEST • AUCKLAND

Harlequin Presents Plus first edition July 1993
ISBN 0-373-11567-9

Original hardcover edition published in 1992
by Mills & Boon Limited

RICH AS SIN

CHAPTER ONE

IT WAS the thumping in his head that woke him. That, and the sour taste in his mouth, which was an unpleasant reminder of the amount of alcohol he had consumed the night before. But what the hell? No one really cared whether he went to bed sober, or drank himself into a senseless stupor. He was unattached: a free agent. No longer the brunt of any woman's dissatisfactions. He could please himself what he did; how he lived. And if the knowledge didn't exactly please him, then tough! Given enough time, he'd get used to it.

Or would he? Rolling over in the tumbled bed, Matthew cast a bleary eye at the clock on the nearby table. God! he grunted ruefully. It was after twelve o'clock! No wonder his head was thumping. As he hadn't eaten a thing since noon the previous day, he was probably starving as well as dehydrating.

Still, he defended himself, as he hauled himself into an upright position and sat for a moment, waiting for the sledgehammer in his skull to slow its pace, he had been working until after midnight. The new program he was devising was probably going to outsell all his other programs, and he shouldn't be too hard on himself if he used alcohol as a stimulant. The fact that he hadn't needed that kind of stimulation until Melissa walked out on him was something he preferred not to remember. Time would deal with Melissa as it had dealt with everything else. And at least he had his work to alleviate his misery.

Pushing himself to his feet, he paused again before lurching across the expensive shag-pile carpet to the bathroom. After attending to his most immediate needs, he leaned on the porcelain basin and viewed his stubbled features without enthusiasm. His eyes were bloodshot; there was a distinctly unhealthy tinge of greyness in his skin; and, to cap it all, it was two days since he had shaved, so that he resembled nothing so much as a derelict, one of those homeless vagrants who wandered around the country looking for hand-outs.

Which was probably unfair to them, reflected Matthew drily, rubbing a hand over his bristling jawline. At least they had a reason for looking the way they did. He had a decent home, and an occupation, and, because of his maternal grandfather's business acumen, more money than he knew what to do with. No reason at all to behave like an alcoholic, and certainly no reason to look like one.

Grimacing, he turned away from the mirror and stepped into the shower stall. Deliberately ignoring the temperature control, he allowed a stream of cold water to cascade down on to his shuddering body. God! For a moment, the iciness of it almost stopped his breath. But then, squeezing shower gel on to his hands, he began to lather himself fiercely, abrading his protesting flesh, as the water pummelled his head and shoulders.

He felt marginally better when he stepped out of the marble-tiled stall, and wrapped a huge cream bath-sheet about him. His head was still throbbing, but the dragging feeling of lethargy had dissipated somewhat. He didn't feel good, and he knew better than to believe that he would improve as the day wore on. But at least he was awake and active. And the computer keyboard would take care of the rest.

His razor beckoned, and with a sigh of resignation he picked it up. He wouldn't suit a beard, anyway, he consoled himself, as he concentrated on not turning his face into a mess of bloody cuts. Which wasn't easy, when his hand tended to shake at the most inopportune moments. God, he should have had a drink before he started this. It was amazing how a shot of Scotch could stabilise his senses.

He managed to finish the job without creating too much havoc, and dropped the towel on to the cold tiles of the bathroom floor. Then, after another ironic grimace at his appearance, he walked back into the bedroom, wrinkling his nose at the sour smell of alcohol that hit him. Indifferent to the fact that he was naked, and the temperature outside somewhere in the low forties, Matthew unlatched the windows to his balcony and threw them open. Then, after withstanding the blast of cold air that hit him with what he considered was admirable fortitude, he groped for his denims and pulled them on.

He was rummaging in his closet for a clean polo shirt when there was a knock at the bedroom door. Turning, he surveyed the closed door for fully fifteen seconds without answering, and then, stifling his impatience, he called, 'Yeah? What do you want?'

The door opened, just a crack, and a man's bald head appeared. 'Oh,' he said, when he saw Matthew. 'You're up, sir. Will you be wanting some breakfast?'

Matthew's mouth compressed. 'At half-past twelve, Jeeves? I don't think so. I'll just have a sandwich. I want to get to work.'

The door widened to admit the intruder, a huge, giant of a man, whose massive shoulders and straining paunch were constrained beneath navy blue worsted and spotless white linen. The uniform of a gentleman's gentleman sat oddly on such a big man's shoulders, but Matthew knew better than to suggest an alternative. The other man was proud of his appearance.

'Are you going to the office, sir?' he enquired, his sharp eyes taking in the open balcony doors and the untidy state of the bedroom. 'And I wish you wouldn't call me Jeeves, Mr Putnam. I don't like it, and you know it.'

Matthew gave the man a resigned look, and then, having no luck in finding a clean shirt, he reached for the sweatshirt he had discarded the night before. 'No, I don't plan to go into the office today,' he was beginning, when the manservant snatched the sweatshirt out of his hands. 'For God's sake, Victor, what the hell do you think you're doing?'

'Well, judging by your appearance, I'd guess you'd just had a shower, sir,' declared Victor mildly, 'and I'm sure you didn't intend to wear this rather—odorous—item. You have a whole drawer full of clean shirts in the closet behind you. Just tell me what you want, and I'll get it out for you.'

'I can dress myself, thank you—Creighton,' drawled Matthew, with rather less patience. 'Why don't you get out of here until I'm finished? Go and make some coffee or something. I don't need a nursemaid.'

'Did I say you did?' Victor rolled the offending sweatshirt into a ball, and stood his ground. 'But, as it happens, you look as if you need someone's assistance. Your mother isn't going to like this. She's not going to like it at all.'

'My mother?' Matthew paused in the act of choosing a shirt from the drawer Victor had indicated, and turned to look at him again. 'What does my mother have to do with anything?'

'Have you forgotten? You're meeting her for lunch in a little over half an hour.'

'Oh, God!' Matthew slammed the drawer with his hip, and pulled a black polo shirt over his head. The sombre colour only accentuated the pallor of his olive skin, and Victor's tongue clicked his disapproval. But Matthew was indifferent to anyone's feelings but his own at that moment, and the prospect of eating lunch with his mother and enduring her condemnation of his lifestyle was enough to make him wish he'd stayed in bed.

'A sandwich, you said, sir,' murmured Victor, evidently deciding it would be politic to give his employer a breathing space, and Matthew cast him a brooding look.

'Nothing to eat,' he snarled, the jaw he had shaved so inexpertly clenched aggressively. 'Just fetch me a beer, and no arguments. Oh, and call me a cab. With a bit of luck there won't be any available.'

Victor paused in the doorway, his broad features showing his dismay. 'I can drive you, Mr Putnam,' he protested, but his employer's face was adamant.

'I said I'll take a cab,' Matthew retorted. 'Just do it, Victor. And hurry up with that beer!'

Three-quarters of an hour later, Matthew stepped out of the minicab and bent to shove a five-pound note into the driver's hand. 'Thanks,' he said, without meaning it, waving away the change the man would have given him. Then, with a tight smile at the doorman's proffered greeting, he vaulted up the steps and through the swing glass doors into the Ritz's elegant foyer.

The dining-room was at the far end of the hallway, but guests took pre-luncheon drinks in the gilded splendour of the Palm Court. It was there Matthew knew he would find his mother, delicately sipping the Perrier water which was all she allowed herself in the middle of the day. Caroline Putnam—née Apollonius—guarded her appearance with almost as much reverence as her son disregarded his, and it was her proud boast that her wedding dress fitted her as well today as it had done more than thirty years ago.

Of course, the fact that the marriage she had worn the wedding dress for had lasted a considerably shorter time she considered of little consequence. She had married Joseph Putnam when she was only eighteen, much against her parents' wishes, and had soon come to realise her father had been right all along. A penniless Englishman, of good stock but little business acumen, Joseph Putnam had lingered only long enough to sire their only offspring, before taking off on a round-the-world yacht-race that had ended in disaster off the Cape of Good Hope. Of course, Caroline had been suitably grief-stricken when the news was delivered, but no one could deny she had been relieved. It had saved her the publicity—and the expense—of a messy divorce, and Aristotle Apollonius—who preferred the sobriquet of Apollo, for obvious reasons—had been more than willing to take his errant daughter, and her small son, back to Greece.

But, from Matthew's point of view, it had not been an entirely satisfactory solution. Despite the fact that 'Apollo' had had only one child, Caroline, and that therefore Matthew was the only heir to the enormous shipping fortune he had amassed, the boy grew up with a regrettable dislike of his grandfather's use of his money. The politics of power didn't interest Matthew; he saw no merit in controlling people's lives for purely personal gain. And, because his father had left sufficient funds for him to be educated in England, at the same schools he himself had attended, where a spartan regime went hand in hand with a distinct need for self-preservation, he had acquired a cynical aversion towards wealth in all its forms. It was a constant bone of contention between Matthew and the other members of his family, and the fact that he had made his home in England was no small contribution to the continuing discord.

Which was why Matthew was not looking forward to this particular lunch with his mother. Ever since the split with Melissa she had been trying, so far unsuccessfully, to persuade him to come back to Athens. Despite the fact that he had now formed his own company, specialising in computer software, and had no interest in taking his place on the board of the Apollonius Shipping Corporation, Caroline persisted in pursuing her goal.

The trouble was, Matthew was very much afraid that sooner or later she might succeed. He might be able to evade the issue so long as his grandfather was alive, but Apollo was over seventy years old. In ten years, twenty at the most, he was going to die, and then what excuse would he have for avoiding his responsibilities? Whether he liked it or not, hundreds—*thousands*—of people relied on the Apollonius Shipping Corporation for their livelihoods, and there was no way he could sit back and let his grandfather's relatives jealously tear to shreds what he had achieved.

The head waiter recognised him as he climbed the steps into the brightly lit atrium. It might be a dismal early April day outside, but the Palm Court of the London Ritz was as cheerfully brilliant as ever.

'Good morning, Mr Putnam,' the man said, his eyes moving from Matthew to the elegantly dressed woman at a corner table. 'Your mother is waiting for you.'

'Yes, thanks.' Matthew bestowed another brief smile, and started across the room. 'Oh—bring me a Scotch and soda, will you? I see my mother's already on the soft stuff.'

The waiter smiled, and moved away, and Matthew continued on to where his mother was seated on a striped couch. 'Mama,' he greeted her formally, bending to brush his lips against hers. 'Sorry I'm late.'

Caroline Putnam viewed her son with reproof mingled with reluctant pride. Tall, like his father, and dark, like his maternal forebears, Matthew attracted attention wherever he went. Particularly female attention, Caroline admitted, somewhat irritably. Not surprisingly, he had the lean good looks that had attracted her to Joseph Putnam in the first place, but the weaknesses she had not initially recognised in his father had been more than compensated for by her own father's genes. Matthew might not want to accept it, but he was far more like his grandfather than he would admit. He was arrogant, and stubborn, and absurdly independent. He made arbitrary decisions, and expected other people to abide by them. And, allied to that, he had the hooded eyes and muscled strength of a predator: an irresistible combination of sensuality and brute strength.

But he was letting himself go, thought Caroline tersely, viewing the slight thickening of his midriff that swelled above his belt. And jeans, and a leather jerkin! To have lunch with his mother! It was all that bitch Melissa's fault. Announcing she had fallen in love with someone else! Probably because Matthew had been in no hurry to take her to the altar.

'I should have thought you'd have had plenty of time to arrange your schedule so you wouldn't be late,' she remarked now, the attractive accent she still retained taking a little of the sharpness out of her tone. 'I know you haven't been into the office. I called earlier, and Robert told me you were not there.'

'No.' Matthew's response was hardly satisfactory. 'So—when did you arrive?'

'Here—or in England?' Caroline enquired in a clipped voice, jewelled fingers toying with the triple string of cultured pearls that encircled her slender throat, and Matthew's mouth took on a lazy slant.

'In England,' he replied, humouring her. 'I imagine you're occupying your usual suite upstairs.'

'Yes, and you might have taken the trouble to arrive in time to escort me down,' retorted his mother, the dark eyes she had passed on to her son flashing angrily. 'Honestly, Matt, I think you go out of your way to humiliate me! Leaving me sitting here alone! What if some undesirable lout had approached me?'

'The Ritz doesn't admit undesirable louts,' remarked Matthew mildly, nodding his thanks as his Scotch and soda was delivered to the table. 'You could sit here all day and no one would trouble you. But—I admit I should have phoned. As I said before, I'm sorry.'

Caroline sniffed, but her expression had softened somewhat, and although she observed the enthusiasm with which her son swallowed half his drink her reaction was more resigned than censorious.

'Oh, well,' she said, taking a sip of the iced spa water in her glass, 'you're here now, and that's what really matters. For myself, I arrived last evening, and went straight off to that charity gala at the Albert Hall. Your Uncle Henry escorted me. Aunt Celia is still indisposed.'

Matthew nodded. His uncle's wife had never enjoyed the best of health, although he privately believed that her many illnesses were self-induced. It was commonly known that Henry Putnam was inclined to enjoy the company of the opposite sex rather too well, and poor Aunt Celia had paid the price of being too trusting. Nevertheless, from his mother's point of view, the situation could not have been more convenient. She had a ready escort, whenever she needed one, without the complications that an unfettered relationship might have created for someone in her position.

'You, I imagine, were combing the less salubrious nightspots of the city,' she added, as Matthew's summoning of the waiter for a second drink reactivated her impatience. 'Matt, don't you think you're behaving rather foolishly? For heaven's sake, if you were so besotted with the girl, why didn't you marry her, instead of just—sleeping with her?'

Matthew's mouth flattened. 'You know what I think about marriage,' he answered, after issuing further instructions to the waiter. 'Just leave it, will you, Mama? I'll go to hell my own way, if you don't mind. Now—tell me why you wanted to see me. Or was it just to voice your disapproval—yet again?'

'Of course not.'

Caroline uncrossed her silk-clad legs and then re-crossed them again in the other direction. Watching her, Matthew had no difficulty in understanding why his father's brother was so willing to squire her around. At forty-eight, Caroline looked ten years younger, and Matthew was quite prepared to believe that anyone here today who didn't know them would automatically assume he was her lover, not her son.

'You know it's your grandfather's birthday at the end of the month, don't you?' she went on now, and Matthew's dark brow ascended in disbelief.

'So it is,' he agreed, after a moment's thought. 'I'd forgotten. How old is the old devil? Seventy-one?'

'He's seventy-two, actually,' declared Caroline flatly. 'If you remember, you couldn't come to his seventy-first birthday because it clashed with—with Melissa's parents' anniversary ball or something. In any event,' she hurried on, not wanting to linger over unwelcome memories, 'we'd like you to join the family for the celebrations. Apollo's inviting everyone, and it will look rather odd if you're not there.'

Matthew regarded his mother tolerantly over the rim of his glass. 'As it did last year, you mean?'

'No.' Caroline sighed. 'Last year wasn't so important to him!' she exclaimed irritably. And then, as if regretting her candour, she added, 'Never mind about last year. Will you come?'

Matthew frowned. 'What's so special about this year?'

'Well—he's a year older, for one thing...'

'And?'

'And—and—he's not been well,' admitted his mother reluctantly. 'You know how he's always had trouble with his chest. I think it's been a little more troublesome than usual, and it's made him aware of his own mortality.'

Matthew's mouth turned down. 'If he stopped smoking those damned cigars, he might give his respiration system a chance. How many does he get through in a day? Fifteen? Twenty?'

'Oh, not as many as that, surely!' Caroline looked appalled. 'In any case, Apollo would say that if he couldn't live his life the way he wanted to live it, there wouldn't be much point in going on.'

'Hmm.' Matthew could see the subject upset her, and decided to desist. 'Well, I don't know about this birthday bash. You know family parties aren't my style.'

Caroline snorted. 'The way I hear it, social gatherings of any kind aren't your style! You've become a hermit, Matt. A recluse. You don't go anywhere—except into the office occasionally—you don't see anyone——'

'And where've you got all this information from?' enquired Matthew wearily. 'No, don't tell me. I can guess. The admirable Victor!'

'I—may have had the few odd words with your major-domo when I called——'

'I'll bet!'

'—but you know Victor cares about you, too. He wouldn't tell me anything if he didn't think it was in your best interests.'

'Really?'

'Yes, really.' His mother gave a resigned sigh. 'Matt, I don't want to interfere——'

'Then don't.'

'—but I care about you as well. And—and I do wish you'd get this—this infatuation for Melissa Mainwaring out of your system.'

'Right.' Matthew lifted a hand to summon the waiter again. 'Shall we look at the menu?'

Caroline opened her mouth to make a protest, and then closed it again. What was the use? she asked herself impotently, feeling all the pangs of frustrated mother-love as her son turned to speak to the restaurant manager. Matthew was such an attractive man; he had everything to live for. Yet he was allowing a spoilt little bitch, who hadn't got an intelligent thought in her empty little head, to tear his life to pieces.

An hour later, as she was enjoying her second cup of coffee, Caroline risked broaching the subject again. As they ate—and she had noticed Matthew had only picked at his food—the conversation had ranged from the previous night's gala to the preparations for the forth-coming birthday celebrations. It had been the kind of conversation she could have had with anyone. Certainly not the intimate tête-à-tête she had hoped to achieve. Which was why she decided to bring Melissa's name back into the proceedings. Like a wound that was festering, her son's infatuation with the woman wouldn't heal un-til it had been thoroughly aired.

'And—when are Melissa and her prince planning to get married?' she enquired tensely. 'They are going to get married, aren't they? I'm sure I read something about it in last week's tabloids.'

Matthew replaced the cup he had been holding back in its saucer. He should have known better than to imagine his mother would leave well alone. And, of course, she was right. There had been a report that Brigadier Alfred Mainwaring's daughter was going to marry the prince of some unpronounceable Eastern European country. The nuptials were planned to take place in June, and no doubt Caroline knew that as well as he did.

'Soon,' he remarked now, meeting his mother's inno-cent gaze with cool deliberation. 'Why? Do you think you'll get an invitation? How would they describe you? Oh, yes. The mother of the best man!'

Caroline's lips tightened. 'Joke if you like, but you are—or rather you would be, if you'd stop feeling sorry for yourself. I never thought a son of mine could behave so mindlessly! Perhaps you are your father's son, after all.'

Matthew's mouth twisted, and with an exclamation of disgust his mother thrust back her chair and got to her feet. 'I'm going to my room,' she declared angrily, and then, conscious of the stir she was creating, she put a steadying hand on the edge of the table. 'Come and see me tomorrow,' she added in an undertone, as if regretting her hasty announcement. 'And think about your grandfather's birthday. Needless to say, he expects you to be there.'

Matthew did think about what his mother had said, as he walked back to his apartment. The luxurious penthouse he had bought with his own money occupied the top floor of a tall block of apartments in Culver Mews in Knightsbridge, and although he knew Victor wouldn't approve Matthew enjoyed the unaccustomed exercise. It reminded him it was too long since he had been to the gym, and that Victor's obsession with his personal protection meant he had too few opportunities to walk anywhere. And, although it was a cold day, with a threat of rain in the air, the daffodils were out in the park, and the early cherry blossom was already appearing on the trees.

It reminded him of what Greece was like at this time of the year, and most particularly Delphus, the island where his grandfather had his home. The sprawling villa where he had spent the early years of his childhood did hold some happy memories for him, and it would be good to see Yannis again, and Nicos, and all the aunts and cousins he remembered from his youth.

But it wasn't just the idea of obeying his finer instincts, and pleasing his mother for once, that occupied his thoughts as he strode past Hyde Park Corner. It was what his mother had said about Melissa that stuck in his mind. And, although thinking of her with Georgio Ivanov still tore his gut, he was unwillingly aware that she had a point. He should have married her when he had the chance. Goodness knew, she had been eager enough to take the plunge. It had been the one sour note in their relationship, that he had been so unwilling to make their association legal. A lack of commitment was how she had put it, on those increasingly frequent occasions when she had accused him of not loving her enough.

Matthew pushed his hands deeper into the pockets of his leather jacket. *Love*! His lips twisted. He doubted Melissa knew the meaning of the word. No one who professed to love someone as much as she had always professed to love him could have fallen out of love so quickly. And he was cynically aware that Melissa's 'love' was more probably available to the highest bidder. Oh, he might have been her first choice, both sexually and financially, but Ivanov was offering marriage, and that all-important ring on her finger.

For himself, he had never felt any urgency to seek that legitimising scrap of paper. What they had had—or rather, what he had thought they had had—was far more binding than a contract that could just as easily be broken. But he was becoming aware that what Melissa had wanted from him was more than his undying devotion. She had wanted security, the kind of security she could only get if he signed on the dotted line.

So, why should he be so surprised? he asked himself now. His parents' marriage had fallen apart as much because his father was unambitious as through any character weakness on his part. He had long since learned how convenient his father's sudden death had proved to be, for, although his mother might sometimes sentimentalise about his passing, she was not her father's daughter for nothing. All his life, the great god Mammon had ruled his family's actions. And he had been a fool to think that Melissa was any different from the rest.

Victor was waiting when the lift doors slid back at the twenty-second floor. As Matthew stepped on to the hushed luxury of the Chinese rug that virtually filled the panelled foyer, the man came to meet him in obvious disapproval.

'You walked,' he declared, brushing drops of rain from the soft fabric of the jacket his employer slung off, with an impatient finger.

'I walked,' agreed Matthew, heading for the inner hallway that led to his study. 'Rob didn't call, did he? He knew I was having lunch with my mother.'

'Mr Prescott didn't call, no,' Victor assured him tersely, and then, with a change of tone, he added, 'But you do have some mail. The lunchtime delivery came while you were out.' He adopted an expectant expression. 'Would you like to see it?'

Matthew paused, with his hand against the panels of his private sanctum. 'Now, what's that supposed to mean?' he enquired shortly. 'You know I always glance through the afternoon mail at dinnertime. It's probably only bills, in any case.' He hesitated. 'Or do you know something I don't?'

A trace of colour invaded Victor's bullish features. 'Now, how would I——?'

'Victor!'

The man sighed. 'Well—there appears to be a letter from Miss Mainwaring,' he admitted nervously. 'I thought you might wish to see it. As—as——'

'As I appear to be drowning in self-pity, right?' suggested Matthew, tamping down the unwilling thought that Melissa might have come to her senses.

'No, sir!' Victor was indignant. 'I just thought——'

'Where is it?'

Matthew couldn't stand the suspense any longer. Even though his common sense told him that if Melissa wanted to come back, she would hardly write him a letter telling him so, he needed the proof. Damn her, he swore savagely. What could she want now?

Victor riffled through the small pile of business letters and advertising material occupying a silver tray placed on a polished, semi-circular hall table. The letter, with its unmistakable scent of rose petals, was at the bottom, and although he was impatient Matthew didn't miss the significance.

'Can I get you some tea, sir?' Victor enquired, as his employer slid his thumb beneath the seal, but Matthew shook his head.

'Nothing, thanks,' he said, heading back towards his study. 'I'll let you know when I'm hungry.'

Victor looked disappointed, but Matthew couldn't help it. He had no idea why Melissa might be writing to him, and the last thing he needed was Victor peering metaphorically over his shoulder. To emphasise this point, he went into the study and closed the door, before withdrawing the letter from its envelope. Then, noticing that his hands were shaking, he uttered another bitter oath.

Indifferent to the somewhat austere familiarity of his surroundings, Matthew rested his shoulder-blades against the door as he scanned the hand-written missive. Melissa's handwriting had never been particularly legible, and in his present agitated state it was difficult to read the scrawling words. But patience eventually won out over stress, and he was able to translate the gist of the message.

Amazingly, it was an invitation. Melissa was writing to ask if he would come to a party she and her fiancé were giving, to celebrate their engagement. Apparently, although the announcement had already been made formally at the dinner her parents had given in their honour, this party was to be a much less formal affair, for close friends and acquaintances.

The air rushed out of Matthew's lungs in a harsh whoosh. For a few moments, he stared at the letter in his hand, as if expecting it to self-destruct in his fingers. And then, tossing it savagely on to his desk, he bent forward to grip the scarred mahogany with clenched fists. My God, he thought disbelievingly, Melissa actually thought he might attend her engagement party! The idea was ludicrous! And insensitive to the point of cruelty.

It took him several minutes, during which time he wished he had asked Victor to fetch him a bottle of Scotch, to recover his composure. He should have known the letter was not going to be good news. Melissa wanted her revenge, and by God, she was determined to get it.

An expletive burst from his lips, and he straightened abruptly, his jaw clenching as he examined how it made him feel. For the first time since she had walked out on him, he felt a healthy sense of resentment. She was deliberately turning the knife in the wound. And she obviously expected him to refuse.

Poor Georgio, Matthew thought grimly. He doubted he knew Melissa had invited her ex-lover to their engagement party. What an irony! But what exactly was Melissa's game?

Of course, it was possible she wanted him back. Matthew's stomach muscles tightened at the thought. But not on the old terms, he acknowledged, with strengthening cynicism. She had made that plain enough when he'd implored her to stay.

So what was she trying to do? Play one lover off against another? He gave a bitter smile. It might be amusing to find out. There had always been a latent sense of masochism in their relationship.

CHAPTER TWO

'BUT why are you doing this?' Paul Webster regarded his fiancée with impatient eyes. 'I thought the café was doing well enough. Why do you need to supplement your income by acting as someone's skivvy?'

'It's not like that.' Samantha Maxwell endeavoured to keep her temper. 'But you have to understand that this is a new departure. And one which, if it's successful, could prove really exciting.'

Paul snorted. 'Exciting? Working every hour God sends!'

'Not *every* hour,' replied Samantha reasonably. 'Just an odd evening here and there. And it's not as if you're going to miss seeing me. You have to visit your clients, and I'll visit mine.'

'Well, I think you're crazy!'

'Yes, I know.' Samantha pushed a strand of toffee-coloured hair behind her ear and tried to concentrate on the shopping list in front of her. But it wasn't easy with Paul baulking her at every turn, persisting in regarding her job as a secondary occupation.

'I mean,' he went on, as if sensing he was pushing her too hard and attempting to be persuasive, 'it's not as if you're a trained chef, or anything. You're an English graduate, Sam. You could be a teacher. Instead of which, you're playing at housewife in someone else's kitchen.'

Samantha's nostrils flared as she looked up. 'I am not playing at housewife,' she retorted sharply. 'And, whether you like it or not, I enjoy what I do. You can't seem to understand that getting this branch of the business going is a real adventure. And it could be just the beginning of a whole new career.'

'Making other people's meals!'

'Catering—for people who don't have the time, or the inclination, to do it themselves.'

'As I said, playing housewife in other people's kitchens.'

'If you want to put it that way.' Samantha was growing tired of the argument. She looked reflectively around the empty café, with its Austrian blinds and gingham tablecloths. 'I'd have thought you'd be glad I was making such a success of the business. After all, it was your idea that I open this place.'

'Yes. Because you didn't know what you wanted to do, when you left university, and the lease was available. If you hadn't voiced some crazy notion of starting a sandwich-round, I doubt if I'd have suggested it.'

'But you did,' Samantha reminded him, straightening a silver condiment set, and adjusting a fan of scarlet napkins. 'And I'm very grateful to you. It's what I've always wanted to do. Only—well, Mum and Dad were keen that I went to university, and they'd worked so hard to send me there, I couldn't disappoint them. I'm not sorry I went. It taught me a lot. Not least, what my priorities are, and what I hope to achieve.'

'Success in business!' Paul shook his head. 'And all this time I thought you wanted to marry me.'

'I do.' Samantha turned to him then, her honey-pale features taut with worry. 'But it's not the only objective in my life. I need a career, Paul. I really do.'

Paul sighed. 'And you think branching out into personal catering is the answer?'

'I don't know. I haven't done enough of it yet to find out. But meeting Jenny like that was a godsend. And the contacts I made at her dinner party are priceless!'

'But they're all in the West End! I don't like the idea of you driving all that way home in the dark!'

'Oh, Paul!' Samantha tilted her head to one side, and then, abandoning her defensive stance, she crossed to where he was sitting, and perched on his lap. 'You don't have to worry about my safety. I'm a perfectly good driver, and in any case the nights are getting lighter.'

'And what happens when the winter comes again?' persisted Paul, though he had softened sufficiently to nuzzle her neck with his lips. 'Still, we'll be married by then, won't we? You'll have more than your hands full looking after me.'

'Mmm.'

Samantha's response was doubtful, but Paul was too busy nibbling her ear to notice. Nevertheless, when his hand moved to the buttoned fastening of her shirt, she stopped him. It wasn't that she didn't love Paul; she did. But, unlike him, she couldn't switch moods so completely. And she didn't share his willingness to use sex to mend their differences.

'Hey——'

Her protective grip on the lapels of her shirt brought a grunt of protest, but Samantha slid lightly off his knee, and adopted a rueful smile.

'Do you realise what time it is?' she exclaimed, running a nervous palm down the seam of her neat black skirt. 'I've got to call at the wholesaler's before I go home, and if I don't hurry they'll be closed before I get there.'

Paul regarded her dourly for a moment and then, as if controlling his impatience, he rose obediently to his feet. He was a tall man, solid and handsome, in a blond, Nordic sort of way. He liked outdoor activities, and played rugby regularly, which accounted for his rather stolid appearance. He liked to think he was very fit, though Samantha knew he sank rather too many beers in the clubhouse after the match to be in really good shape. Nevertheless, he was kind, and fairly even-tempered, and extremely loyal. And Samantha had known him for over six years, ever since they first got to know one another at the local sixth-form college.

'You know,' he said now, taking a strand of her hair between his thumb and forefinger, and smoothing out its curl, and Samantha's heart sank. 'I must be the only man in Northfleet whose girlfriend is still a virgin. Whose *fiancée* is still a virgin,' he corrected himself heavily. 'Am I going to have to wait until our wedding night, Sam? Is that why you won't let me touch you?'

Samantha suppressed an inward groan, and reached for her jacket, which had been lying over the back of a nearby chair. 'I do let you touch me,' she protested, wishing Paul hadn't chosen this minute to start another conversation about their relationship. 'But we've only been engaged for a little over a month. Give me time. Let me get used to the idea.'

Paul's mouth tightened. 'I could say that you shouldn't have to "get used" to the idea,' he retorted, with rather more heat. 'For God's sake, Sam, it's almost the twenty-first century! As you're so fond of reminding me, women want to be equal with men!'

'Intellectually equal, not sexually,' she countered, pushing her arms into the sleeves of her jacket. Her nail caught on the lining as she did so, and she emitted a sharp gasp of frustration. 'Not now, Paul, please. I'm simply not in the mood.'

'Sometimes I wonder if you ever will be,' he muttered, and although she had only heard the tone of his mumbled protest Samantha swung round.

'What?'

'Forget it.' Paul wound his club scarf around his neck and headed towards the door. 'So—when is this party supposed to be? And who did you say it was for?'

Samantha checked that all the lights were out and that the alarm was set, and followed him outside. 'It's an engagement party,' she answered, locking the door behind them. 'It's next Tuesday, at a house in Eyton Gate. I dealt with someone called Lederer, but I think he was just a secretary or something.'

'Eyton Gate, eh?' Paul pulled a wry face, as they crossed the pavement to where his car was waiting. 'You're really hitting the big time, aren't you?'

'I hope so.' Samantha endeavoured to sustain the feeling of excitement she had felt when she'd taken the call. 'So—I'll see you tomorrow, yes?'

'If my mother's cooking isn't too simple for you,' remarked Paul caustically, swinging open the car door, and Samantha sighed.

'Will you stop this?' she exclaimed. 'Can't you at least find it in your heart to be pleased that I'm making some progress? I don't want to be a waitress all my life.'

'I don't want you to be a waitress all your life either,' he retorted, levering his bulk behind the wheel of the sporty little Mazda. Then, with a shrug, he reached out and grabbed her hand. 'OK. I guess I am pleased for you, really. Just don't get too high-powered, will you? Or you may decide you don't want to marry a hard-working estate agent, after all.'

'Since when are estate agents hard-working?' queried Samantha, her smile mirroring her relief. 'OK, I promise I won't. Now, I must go, or the wholesaler's really will be closed.'

Paul nodded, and Samantha waited until he had driven away before crossing the road to where her own Mini van was parked. Although the back of the van was fitted with shelves to transport the food she prepared at home, she reflected that she would have to get a small transit if she planned to expand into catering in a big way. It was all very well using the Mini when all she did was ride back and forth from home, with an occasional trip to the Cash and Carry. But travelling the fifty or so miles from this small Essex town to London and back was going to put a definite strain on her capabilities. Particularly as sometimes she might have to take Debbie with her.

Her mother had a meal waiting when she finally got home. Although she worked with food all day, Samantha seldom ate anything at the café. Besides, the little restaurant closed at five-thirty, and by the time Samantha and her assistant, Debbie Donaldson, had scoured all the equipment, cleaned the dining-room and spread fresh cloths on the tables, she was quite happy to let someone wait on her for a change.

'You look tired,' said Mrs Maxwell frankly, setting a plate of home-made steak and kidney pie in front of her daughter, and Samantha's lips twisted.

'Do I?' she said. 'Thank you. That's all I wanted to hear.'

'Well, you do,' declared her mother, seating herself across from her daughter and viewing the smudges beneath the younger woman's eyes with some concern. 'What have you been doing until this time? Your father and your sister had their meal over an hour ago. Don't blame me if yours is dried up. It's been in the oven since half-past six.'

Samantha smiled. 'It's fine,' she said, unenthusiastically forking a mouthful of limp pastry into her mouth. 'And you know I had to go to the wholesaler's. I told you that this morning.'

'Until this time?'

'Well— I was late leaving.' Samantha moistened her lips. 'Paul came round just after we closed.'

'Ah.' Mrs Maxwell didn't sound surprised. 'And what did he have to say?'

Samantha grimaced. 'Can't you guess?'

'He's not happy about you doing these private dinner parties, is he? And quite honestly, I don't blame him.'

'Oh, Mum!'

'Don't "Oh, Mum" me. You know how we feel about it. Your Dad and I, that is. I wish you'd never met that Jennifer Gregory again. She's unsettled you, and I can't forgive her for that.'

'Mum, I met Jenny at university, remember? And it was your and Dad's idea that I go there. And her name's Spellman now, not Gregory. And whatever you say, I think she's provided me with a marvellous opportunity.'

'To cook for someone else. To be a servant, in someone else's home.'

'No!' Samantha gasped. 'You're beginning to sound like Paul. It's not like that. I just do the catering, that's all. It's what I do, Mum. What do you think running a café is all about?'

'The café's yours—or you pay the lease, anyway, thanks to that insurance your grandmother left you.'

'And I'll still be running the café, as well as providing a catering service for anyone who can afford me.'

'Hmm.' Mrs Maxwell didn't sound impressed. 'And do they know—these friends of Jenny's, I mean—that you're not a professional caterer?'

'I *am* a professional caterer.'

'I don't think a night school diploma is the same as real professional experience,' persisted her mother. 'They probably think you've worked in some top London restaurant. I wonder what they'd say if they saw the Honey Pot?'

'I don't particularly care,' exclaimed Samantha, pushing her barely touched plate aside. 'But thanks for your support. It's what I really needed. Now, if you don't mind, I'll go and take a shower.'

Mrs Maxwell sighed. 'I'm sorry,' she said, as her daughter got up from the table. 'Perhaps I was a little harsh. But I worry about you, Sam, I do honestly. Don't you think you have enough on, running the café practically single-handed, without taking on more work, to add to the burden?'

Samantha hesitated. 'It doesn't occur to you that I'm going to be paid far more for the catering than I'll ever earn in the café, does it? I don't want to give up the café. I want to improve it. And, if I'm successful, I may be able to afford a full-time cook to work in the kitchen. That way, we could expand the menu, both for the café and the catering service.'

Her mother frowned. 'Well, what does Paul say?'

'Paul just wants me to go on running the café until we get married. Then—who knows? I don't think he envisages me continuing with my career much beyond the first year.'

Mrs Maxwell sighed. 'Well, that doesn't sound unreasonable to me. And, after all, until you met Jennifer Greg—Spellman again, you seemed happy enough doing what you were doing. Then she tells you she's giving a dinner party, and that her caterers have let her down at the last minute, and before we know it you're dashing off to London, and getting these big ideas.'

'Mum, the dinner party was a huge success! Everyone said so. And, believe it or not, good caterers are worth their weight in gold to these people. Times are changing. The days when people could afford to employ a full-time cook are long-gone. Besides, people don't want to do that kind of work nowadays; not for someone else, anyway,' she added hastily. 'That's why people like me are in such demand. We come in, we cook the meal, and we go away again. And it's much more intimate than taking your guests to a restaurant.'

Mrs Maxwell shook her head. 'All the same, I don't think even you imagined what would happen?'

'The phone calls, you mean?' Samantha gave a rueful smile. 'No, I didn't. But isn't it exciting? I could probably work *every* night of the week, if I wanted.'

'But you're not going to?' Her mother looked alarmed.

'No, I've told you.' Samantha paused. 'To begin with, I'm only going to take on one, maybe two nights' work in any week. Then, we'll see how it goes. At the moment, all I want to think about is next Tuesday's engagement party.'

'In Mayfair.'

'Well, it's Belgravia, actually,' said Samantha evenly. 'But yes. It's in the West End. Apparently the female half of the happy couple is a friend of Jenny's. And they're having the party at her fiancé's house.'

Mrs Maxwell shook her head. 'Well, you watch out, Sam. These people aren't like us, you know, and you being an attractive girl and everything—just watch your step.'

Samantha smiled. 'Yes, Mum.'

'Well, you can laugh. But it's true. Some people think money can buy anything.'

Samantha's expression softened. 'I know,' she said, recognising her mother's very real fears on her behalf. 'But I am twenty-four, you know. I know what I'm doing.'

After popping her head round the living-room door to offer a belated greeting to her father and her younger sister Penny, Samantha trudged up the stairs to her room. She was tired. She freely admitted it. But it was more a mental tiredness, born of the arguments she had had with both Paul and her mother, than any physical weakness on her part. It was so hard to make them understand how she felt about this latest development in her career. When she left university, it was true, she had no serious plans for her future. Oh, she had always liked messing about in the kitchen, and trying new recipes on the family, but she had just regarded that as a hobby, until her father had put the idea of starting a sandwich-round into her head.

As the manager of a jeweller's in the High Street, Mr Maxwell had got into the habit of going into the local pub for a sandwich at lunchtime, but, as he said, he didn't always want the beer that went with it. He had encouraged Samantha when she had put forward her idea of using her car to deliver home-made sandwiches all over town, and Paul's offer of the lease on what had previously been a rather sleazy café had just been an extension of that. She had still provided sandwiches, but her clients had had to come to her for them, and pretty soon she had branched out into quiches, and salads, and home-made cakes and scones. The Honey Pot had taken off, and during the past two years it had gone from strength to strength. She even employed a full-time as-

sistant now, and her account books were beginning to
show a healthy profit. But this latest development was
something else, and it was hard to be enthusiastic when
everyone else thought she was getting out of her depth.

Standing in the shower, she avoided looking at her reflection in the walls of the Perspex stall. She was half
afraid of what she might see in the dark-fringed depths
of her eyes, eyes that could change from green to grey,
according to her mood. Was she being too ambitious? she
wondered, scooping gel from the bottle and lathering her
damp hair. Was that what Paul was afraid of? She had
never thought of herself as being so, but she couldn't
deny she was excited. She would have to think of a name
for the new service, she thought, determinedly putting all
negative thoughts aside. Not the Honey Pot again. That
belonged to the café. So how about 'Honey Home-
maker', just to keep the connection?

The buffet looked perfect, even if Samantha had had a
few small set-backs at the beginning. Finding that one of
the smoked salmon mousses had lost its shape on the
journey had been a minor disaster, but happily she had
prepared more than she needed, and that obstacle had
been overcome.

Then Miss Mainwaring, her employer's fiancée, had
thrown a paddy because there was no caviare. A buffet
wasn't a buffet without caviare, she had exclaimed, and
it had taken a great deal of effort on her fiancé's behalf
to persuade her that it really wasn't important.

He had been nice, Samantha reflected, as she gathered her belongings together, preparatory to leaving. A
prince, moreover, although his title wasn't one she was
familiar with. But then, she wasn't familiar with these
people at all, she acknowledged ruefully. A fact that had

been made clear to her by Melissa Mainwaring's biting tongue.

All the same, it had been an edifying experience, and she had learned one or two salutory lessons. She had discovered, for instance, that it was far harder to organise a buffet than it was to arrange a formal sit-down dinner. And luck had played a part in saving her from ruining this unique opportunity. It hadn't occurred to her, until she was unloading the pizza, that it was no use providing hot food when you couldn't be assured the guests would eat to order. But thankfully her pizzas tasted just as good cold as hot, and instead of offering them in slices, as she had originally intended, she cut the juicy wedges into bite-sized squares, easily handled on the end of a cocktail spear.

Happily, the rest of the food offered no problems. Her tarts and quiches looked appetisingly rich against the backcloth of finely embossed damask. And Samantha threaded strands of asparagus fern between the plates of meats and salads, adding scarlet rosebuds to enhance the luscious trifles. When she left the tables to go downstairs and pack up, there was already a satisfying group of guests admiring her efforts. She just hoped everything tasted as good as it looked. One other difference between the buffet and a formal dinner was that she didn't stay around long enough to find out.

Which was a pity, because she'd enjoyed working in this kitchen. With its quarry-tiled floor, and solid mahogany fittings, it reminded her of pictures she had seen of Victorian kitchens. However, no Victorian kitchen had ever had its standards of cleanliness, or provided such a wealth of gadgets to make cooking here a pleasure.

Upstairs had been impressive, too. Dividing doors had been rolled back to create a huge reception area, and although Samantha had only had a glimpse of the linen-hung walls and high carved ceilings as she and the waiters, hired for the occasion, carried the food up from the kitchen, it had been enough. Evidently, whatever else he was, Prince Georgio was not a member of some impoverished aristocracy. On the contrary, he must be extremely rich—and Miss Mainwaring probably knew it.

An unkind conclusion, Samantha reproved herself severely, as she packed plates and dishes back into the cold-boxes she had brought them in. After all, she knew nothing about Melissa Mainwaring, except that she was a friend of Jenny's, and she was fond of caviare. And if she, Samantha, wanted to make a success of this business, she had to try and get on with everybody. Even spoilt little rich girls who enjoyed making scenes!

She was so intent on what she was doing, so absorbed with her thoughts, that when she turned and saw the man leaning against the tall freezer she started violently. She had thought she was alone, all the waiters hired for the evening busy circulating the champagne upstairs. But in the next instant she realised that this man was no waiter, and in the same breath she saw the half-open door behind him.

Until then, she hadn't noticed the rear entry. The house, one of a row of terraced Georgian properties, had been designed to provide living accommodation on its three upper floors. The lower ground floor, where Samantha was now, was entered by means of area steps at the front of the house, and it had never occurred to her that there might be a back entrance on this level. Or that it might be unlocked.

Her mouth drying, she looked at the man with anxious eyes. Who was he? she wondered. A servant? A *thief*? He didn't look entirely English, and although he wasn't heavily built, like Paul, there was a muscular hardness to his lean body. She supposed he was about six feet; again, not as tall as Paul, but more powerfully masculine. His dark hair needed cutting, and there was a film of stubble on his chin. It added to the air of toughness and alienation that exuded from him, an aura that was strengthened by the fact that he was dressed totally in black.

Swallowing, Samantha decided she had no choice but to bluff it out. There was no way she could get round the table and make it to either of the other two doors without him catching her. Something told her he would move just as swiftly as the predator he resembled, but perhaps he would leave her alone if he thought she was no threat to him.

'I—er—the party's not down here,' she said, stifling an exclamation as her shaking hands clattered two quiche plates together. God! She was trying not to do anything to agitate him. At this rate, he'd soon guess that she was scared rigid.

But, 'I know,' he remarked, in a laconic voice, making no move to budge from his lounging position. 'I'm sorry if I startled you,' he added. 'I assumed everyone would be upstairs. I imagine Ivanov's guests have arrived by now, haven't they?'

Samantha blinked. *Ivanov's* guests! So he knew whose house it was, then. Did that make it better or worse? She was too shocked to make a decision.

And his voice disturbed her. It had a low gravelly edge that scraped across her nerves. Yet it was a cultivated voice, as well. Hoarse, but not the broad London accent she would have expected.

He moved then and, in spite of herself, she flinched. She didn't quite know what she expected him to do, but when her eyes alighted on the knife she had used to cut the pizza lying on the table beside her, her fingers flexed automatically.

'I guess you're wondering what I'm doing here,' he began, his lips twisting half sardonically, and Samantha took a choking breath. His upper lip was quite thin, she noticed inconsequently, but the lower one was full and sensual. The mark of a sensitive nature, she wondered wildly, or simply an indication of brute strength?

'I—it's nothing to do with me,' she said, aware that her voice had risen half an octave. She edged one of the cold-boxes forward so that it hid the knife from his view. Then, as her fingers closed around the handle, 'Is—is Mr Ivanov expecting you?'

A faint smile touched his mouth. His lips parted to reveal even white teeth, and his tongue appeared to dampen a corner in a decidedly amused gesture. '*Mr* Ivanov?' he echoed, as Samantha's scattered senses registered the powerful attraction of that smile. 'I gather you don't know him very well.'

Samantha's lips tightened. Did he mean because she hadn't addressed him as *Prince* Ivanov? Or simply because she had said *Mr* Ivanov?

'I—don't,' she declared, realising he hadn't answered her question. Her fingers took a firmer hold on the knife. 'Wh-why don't you go up and see him?'

It was a calculated risk she was taking. She had no idea what he might do when confronted with a roomful of Prince Georgio's guests, but at least it would give her a chance to call the police. And there was no point in trying to be a hero—a *heroine*—when he was so much taller and stronger than she was. She might find the courage to use the knife to defend herself, but she couldn't see herself using it to stop him from invading the party. Indeed,

the very idea of sinking its cruel blade into his yielding
flesh was enough to bring her out in a cold sweat.

'Yes,' he said now, pushing his hands into the pockets
of his leather jacket, 'why don't I do that?' But then,
dispelling the feeling of relief that his words had kin-
dled, his heavy lids narrowed the penetration of eyes so
dark, they seemed as black as his outfit. 'So what are you
doing down here?'

'Me?' It was almost a squeak, and Samantha cleared
her throat before continuing. 'I——' It was still too high,
and she consciously tried to lower her tone. 'I—I'm just
the ca-caterer.'

'The caterer?' he echoed, half disbelievingly, and she
realised that in her hip-length sweater and black leggings
she didn't look like anyone's idea of a waitress. But she
had changed out of the neat white blouse and short black
skirt she had worn to set out the buffet tables. In here,
five minutes ago, she remembered, in horror. God! She
should be grateful he hadn't surprised her in her bra and
panties!

'I—yes, the caterer,' she confirmed, the memory of
what could have happened giving her a momentary
respite. 'That—that's what I'm doing. Packing up my
things.'

His frown was thoughtful, drawing his straight black
brows together. He had nice eyebrows, she thought, dark
and vital, like his hair, and his nose was straight and well-
formed, between bones that accentuated the hollows of
his cheeks. Altogether, it was a disturbingly attractive
face, she acknowledged, and then inwardly flayed herself for thinking so. For pity's sake, the man was an intruder, or worse! How could she find him attractive? She
must be losing her mind!

He moved again, approaching the table this time, and all thoughts of his appearance fled. All her old fears flooded back in full measure, and when he put out a hand to examine the nearest cold-box her nerve snapped. Snatching up the knife, she positioned it against her midriff, holding it with both hands, the handle towards her stomach, the blade pointing viciously outwards.

'Don't touch anything!' she cried, unable to hold down her panic any longer. 'Get—get away from the table. Or—or I'll use this. Believe me, I know how.'

His expression was ludicrous. If she hadn't known better, she might almost have believed he was as shocked as she was. He stared at her as if she had really lost her senses, and his hands came out of his pockets to perform a soothing gesture.

'Hey,' he said, 'calm down——'

'Keep away from me!' Samantha was shaking like a leaf, and her hold on the knife was desperate. Her palms were sweating with the knowledge that she had really burned her boats now. She had shown him she didn't trust him, and there was no turning back.

'Please,' he protested, 'put the knife down. You're making a terrible mistake——'

'You made the mistake in coming here,' she retorted, glancing behind her, measuring the distance to the stairs. 'If—if you have any sense you'll get out of here. If you're still here when I get back, the police will   ouch!'

Her words were brought to an abrupt halt when he lunged forward and grabbed her arm. Taking advantage of her momentary lapse in concentration, he grasped her wrist and twisted sharply. The knife fell to the floor with a loud clatter, and before she could turn away he jerked her hard against him.

Her first crazy thought was that she had been right: his body was much harder and tougher than Paul's. And the second was that he was no gentleman. A gentleman wouldn't twist her arm up behind her back until it felt as if it might break, or hold her as if there was some danger of her laying a karate chop across the back of his neck. The only kind of chops she knew about were lamb, and pork, and if it weren't so serious she could almost find it funny.

A sob escaped her, but it was as much a suppression of the hysterical laughter that was bubbling inside her as an expression of pain. Nevertheless, he heard it, and his hold on her arm eased ever so slightly, as he drew back to look down at her.

'Are you crazy, or what?' he demanded, and she was relieved to see he looked no more menacing than he had done a few moments ago. But he had been drinking. She could smell it on his breath.

'You—you ask me that!' she got out, trying to free her other arm that was imprisoned by her side. 'After—after breaking in here!'

'Are you kidding?' He blinked now, and she thought what absurdly long eyelashes he had, for a man. But she was making far too many personal observations about him, and she determinedly schooled her thoughts along with her expression. 'I didn't break in,' he added impatiently. 'Believe it or not, I have an invitation!'

'You do?' Samantha wasn't sure whether she should believe him or not, but as he was holding the upper hand—in more ways than one, she acknowledged painfully—what choice did she have?

'Yes.' He let go of the arm he had been punishing, and transferred his hold to her waist. 'Can I trust you not to pull another stunt like that, if I let you go?'

Samantha's lips trembled, but a smile was tugging at the corners of her mouth. 'I—I think so,' she said, becoming conscious of the underlying intimacy of their situation. Whether he realised it or not, she was acutely aware of his lean hips inclined towards hers, and the muscled thigh that was threatening to part her legs. 'Are you going to? Let me go, I mean,' she appended, as the ambiguity of her words brought an embarrassed wave of colour to her cheeks.

Amazingly, the ebony eyes darkened. Samantha wouldn't have believed they could, and it wasn't so much an increasing definition of colour as a deepening of quality, a softening, that gave the pupils a curious lightness.

'Do you want me to?' he asked, and there was a distinctly husky timbre to his hoarse voice now that caused a feathering of flesh all over her body. Dear heaven, he was sexy, she thought, her senses racing out of control. It wasn't exactly what he was saying, it was the way he was saying it, and her tongue appeared to wet her lips in unknowing invitation.

'I——' she began, knowing how she ought to answer him, but hesitating none the less. And then a voice that she remembered rather too well broke over them in shrill accusation.

'Matt! Matt, is that you? In God's name, what are you doing down here?'

Melissa Mainwaring came down the stairs as she spoke, her short-skirted dress of crisp blue taffeta rustling as she did so. It also slipped enticingly off one white shoulder, drawing attention to the pearly quality of her skin, and the ripe, rounded shape it concealed.

The man stiffened. There was no other way to describe the sudden freezing of his body. With unhurried but nevertheless decisive movements, he released Samantha and stepped back, his expression twisting oddly in the harsh track of a spotlight. It gave her the opportunity to try and gather her own composure, though the expression in Melissa's eyes as she looked at her was not encouraging.

She had reached the bottom of the stairs now, and her high heels rang noisily against the copper-coloured tiles. But, her attention was all on the man beside Samantha now and, although she clearly hadn't liked their earlier closeness, his subsequent withdrawal had mollified her somewhat.

'You came,' she said, her expression changing to one of extreme satisfaction. 'I hoped you would.'

'Did you?'

His response was scarcely enthusiastic, though Samantha sensed that he was holding his real emotions in check. There was a distinct tenseness in the way he held himself, in the way he spoke. Something was going on here, something she knew nothing about, and she wished, with all her heart, that she could escape before his control snapped.

'Yes.' The woman's gaze switched to the girl beside him, and Samantha thought how ironic it was that she and Melissa should have had that altercation earlier. It made the present situation so much more awkward, and she just wanted to pick up her boxes and leave. 'I see Miss Maxwell let you in.'

'I let myself in,' the man contradicted her, but Melissa was not appeased.

'But you know one another,' she probed, crossing her arms across her midriff, and massaging her elbows with delicate hands.

'No.' The man—*Matt*?—shifted his weight from one foot to the other, pushing his hands into the pockets of his leather jacket. 'Miss—Maxwell?' He looked briefly at Samantha, and she quickly bent her head. 'Miss Maxwell thought I was an intruder.'

Melissa frowned. 'Is this true?' she asked, and Samantha sighed.

'Yes.'

'It was my fault for coming in the back way,' declared Matt sardonically. He bent to pick up the knife that still lay glinting on the floor, but although he glanced at Samantha as he did so he made no mention of it. 'So—I believe congratulations are in order. You finally got someone to take the bait.'

If Samantha was shocked by his words, Melissa was more so. 'You—bastard!' she choked, and the look she cast in the other woman's direction was eloquent of the fury she felt at Samantha's being a witness to her humiliation. There would be no useful contacts from this dinner party, not if Melissa had anything to do with it, Samantha thought ruefully. But at the same time she felt a small sense of satisfaction that whatever was going on here, the man—Matt? Matthew?—was apparently quite capable of holding his own.

'I—if you'll excuse me,' she murmured, deciding not to push her luck. It was one thing to be an unwilling witness; it was quite another to become a participant in their quarrel.

Melissa took a deep breath. 'Where are you going?'

Samantha moistened her lips. 'I'm leaving.'

'Like hell you are!' Melissa shot Matthew a crippling glare. 'People haven't even started eating yet. It'll be hours before the tables can be cleared. Go to the bathroom, or somewhere. Mr Putnam and I only need a few moments' privacy.'

'No.' Samantha thrust the last of her belongings into the boxes, and fastened the safety clips. Right now, she didn't particularly care if she smashed all her dishes. She just wanted to get out of there, for more reasons than she cared to consider. 'I—your—that is, the prince knows I only—prepare the food. I don't clean up afterwards.'

'Why not?' Melissa's undoubtedly striking features were less than appealing at this moment. 'You're just a waitress, aren't you? That's what you're doing here.'

'No,' said Samantha again, snatching up her jacket, and grabbing hold of two of the cold-boxes. 'I just—deliver the food, that's all.' It was easier than trying to explain. 'And now, as I say, I must be going. It—it's getting late, and I've got a long way to drive.'

Melissa looked as if she would have liked to try and stop her by force, but, instead, she contented herself with a sarcastic sneer. 'Well, you can tell your employer we weren't very impressed with the service,' she declared spitefully. 'Oh, and mention the caviare, won't you? You have heard of caviare, I assume?'

Samantha gritted her teeth, intensely aware of the man standing listening to the proceedings, with a faintly mocking expression on his dark face. 'I'll remember,' she said tightly, bumping the boxes against the cupboards as she struggled to the door. Just a few more yards, she thought, wondering how she could turn the handle without wasting time putting her boxes down, and then the man intervened.

'Allow me,' he said, reaching past her to pull open the door, and she gave him a grateful smile. 'Drive carefully,' he added, as she hurriedly ascended the steps, but any response she might have made died on her lips. As she glanced behind her, Melissa came to grasp his arm, and drag him back into the kitchen. Samantha's last glimpse was of the two of them standing very close together, and of Melissa's scarlet-tipped fingers spread against his chest.

CHAPTER THREE

THE HONEY POT was hectic, and Samantha was busy microwaving dozens of the individual earthenware dishes of her home-made lasagne when she saw him.

It was odd, that sudden awareness, but she noticed him the moment he entered the café. Afterwards, she told herself it was the stir his leather-clad appearance caused among the bank clerks, shop assistants, and other office workers, who made up the bulk of the lunchtime crowd. But, whatever it was, she knew an unfamiliar sense of panic, as he threaded his way between the tables.

Debbie Donaldson, her assistant, whose job it was to serve the customers and clear the tables, intercepted him before he could reach the refrigerated cabinets, where delicious plates of sandwiches and salads were on display.

'A table for one?' she enquired, her wide blue eyes assessing, taking in his dark attractive features and leanly muscled frame.

'What?' His eyes had been on Samantha, who was hurriedly preparing another of the pre-cooked pasta dishes for the microwave, and trying to pretend she hadn't seen him. 'Oh——' He expelled his breath on an impatient sigh, and glanced briefly round the small restaurant. 'Yes. Why not?' His gaze narrowed to enclose only Debbie. 'Can you fit me in?'

'I'm sure I can.'

Debbie's lips parted to reveal a provocative tongue, and Samantha, unwillingly aware of how impressionable the eighteen-year-old was, felt a surge of raw frustration. What was he doing here? she wondered, stifling a curse as she burned her thumb on a hot dish. He was a long way from Eyton Gate and Belgravia. How on earth had he found her? And who the hell was he anyway?

A surreptitious glance across the room informed her that Debbie had seated him at a small table in the bow window. It was one of the only two tables left vacant in the café, and was usually reserved for Mr Harris, the manager of the local building society. But Debbie wasn't looking her way, so Samantha couldn't signal that that table was unavailable. Debbie's attention was firmly fixed on her customer—as was the attention of most of the females present.

Not that she could blame them, Samantha admitted ruefully, trying to concentrate on what she was doing. He was clean-shaven this morning, and the hooded eyes and stark uncompromising features possessed a potent sensuality. Two sausages, one cannelloni, and two egg and cress sandwiches, she recited silently, struggling to remember the orders. But his presence disturbed her, reminding her as it did of that evening two nights ago, when he had invaded Prince Georgio's kitchen.

She had tried to put the memory of that evening out of her mind. She didn't want to think about her emotions at that time. She had told herself it was natural not to want to dwell on the scare he had given her. But the truth was, her fears had been superseded by the way he had made her feel when he'd disarmed her.

Disarmed her in more ways than one, she thought drily, trying to make light of it. And who would want to remember the things Melissa Mainwaring had said to her? No, the whole evening had been a disaster. She was actually having second thoughts about continuing that particular side of the business.

'He says he wants to speak to you.'

Debbie's vaguely resentful voice rang in her ear, and Samantha stopped spreading the egg and cress mixture on the bread and looked at her assistant.

'Who?' she asked, keeping her back firmly to the tables, and Debbie gave her a disbelieving look.

'Who do you think?' she exclaimed. 'The joker sitting over there by the window. The one doing an imitation of Mel Gibson.'

Samantha blinked, really confused this time. 'Mel Gibson?' she echoed.

'Mad Max?' suggested Debbie shortly, in the tone of one explaining table manners to a five-year-old. 'And don't pretend you didn't see him come in. You and half the female population of Northfleet!'

Samantha expelled her breath, and laid one slice of bread over the other. 'Well—what does he want?' she asked, praying he hadn't told Debbie of their earlier encounter. But the younger girl only shrugged.

'I don't know. He just said he wanted to speak to you. Do you know him? Is he a friend of Paul's?'

'Hardly.' The word was out before Samantha could prevent it, but she covered herself by adding swiftly, 'I ask you: does he look like a friend of Paul's?'

Debbie cast a glance over her shoulder. 'Well, no,' she admitted. 'I can't honestly see Paul buying leather gear, let alone getting into it.' She turned back to look at her employer. 'So what do you think he wants? Protection money?'

Samantha's amused gasp had a trace of hysteria in it. 'Protection money!' she echoed disparagingly. My God!

Debbie had some imagination. She sobered abruptly. But perhaps it wasn't so far-fetched. Maybe she did need protection. From him!

'Well, are you going to go and see what he wants, or aren't you?' Debbie demanded, resentful that her idea had been dismissed so wholeheartedly. 'I suppose he could have a message or something. You know, one of those express delivery services. It's obvious he's come on a motorbike.'

'Is it?'

Now Samantha permitted herself another brief glance in his direction. To her relief, he was looking out of the window and didn't see her. But her own reaction to his lounging figure was no less disruptive because of that.

'I'd say so,' Debbie declared now, edging Samantha aside, and taking over the slicing of the sandwich. 'Go on. You'd better see what he wants. I get the feeling he's not going to go away until he's spoken to you.'

Samantha expelled her breath unevenly, and looked down at her bibbed apron. Her immediate impulse was to take it off, but of course she didn't. So far as she knew, he was here to have lunch just like any other of her customers. He had asked her to serve him because he felt that their previous encounter entitled him to trade on their acquaintance. And besides, she could imagine Debbie's reaction if she attempted to smarten herself up to speak to him. He had already caused enough of a stir by coming here. Paul was bound to hear about it anyway, so why exacerbate an already awkward situation?

In consequence, she felt a certain amount of trepidation as she made her way towards him. The smiles she cast at her regular customers were unusually tight, and the words she did exchange were short and to the point. It wasn't that she never served the customers. On the

contrary, sometimes she and Debbie were both practically run off their feet, particularly at weekends. But this
was different, and she knew it. And with Debbie's eyes
upon her, it was difficult to behave naturally.

He half got out of his seat, as she approached the table, but then, as if realising it wasn't the done thing, he
subsided again. With his arm hooked across the back of
his chair, and his ankle resting easily across his knee, he
lazily resumed his lounging position.

'You'll forgive me for not getting up,' he said, as she
reached the table, and Samantha came to an unwilling
halt.

'What can I get you?' she asked, carefully ignoring his
attempt to be familiar. 'The menu's on the table.'

'So it is.' His eyes flicked carelessly over the plastic clip
that held the printed card. 'What would you recom-
mend?' He glanced about him. 'The lasagne appears to
be popular.'

Samantha thrust her fists into the pouchlike pocket of
her apron. 'What do you want?' she demanded, and they
both knew she was not talking about the menu now. 'I'm
very busy.'

'So I see.' His dark eyes assessed her flushed cheeks,
and the wisps of moist hair that clung to her forehead.
'How long have you been running this place?'

'Two years—if that's any concern of yours.'
Samantha's nervousness was giving way to indignation.
'Look, I don't know why you've come here, but I wish
you hadn't. Now, if you want to eat, OK. Otherwise, I'm
going to have to ask you to vacate this table.'

Humour tugged at the corners of his lips, but he
reached obediently for the menu. 'I'll have—a toasted
cheese sandwich,' he said, after a moment. 'Oh—and a
beer, too. If you have one.'

Samantha was fairly sure he knew they didn't have a licence to serve alcohol, and her nails dug into her palms. 'That'll have to be a fruit juice,' she informed him, resenting the fact that she had no excuse not to serve him. And, remembering he had been drinking the last time she spoke to him, she added tautly, 'Perhaps you'd be better off at the pub!'

'No. I'll stay here,' he responded, setting the menu back on the table. 'Thanks.'

Samantha hesitated, and then, realising she had no further reason to linger, she turned and stamped back into the kitchen. But her normally even-tempered mood was shattered, and Debbie eyed her warily as she slapped two slices of bread under the grill.

'What did he say?' she asked, after a moment, curiosity getting the better of her, and Samantha cast her a scowling glance.

'Nothing,' she replied at last, realising she was going the right way to arouse the girl's suspicions. 'He wants a toasted cheese sandwich and a glass of orange juice. You can take it to him.'

'Me?' Debbie looked surprised, and Samantha couldn't blame her. 'So why did he ask for you to serve him?'

'Who knows?' Samantha flipped the bread over, and reached for the cheese. 'Go and see if any tables need clearing. As you've commandeered Mr Harris's table, you'll have to find somewhere else to put him when he comes in.'

Debbie pressed her lips together. 'Are you sure you're all right, Sam?' she persisted, evidently feeling some responsibility for what had happened, and not happy with the result. 'You look—sort of upset.'

'Don't be silly, Debbie.' Samantha managed a faint smile, as she covered the bread with cheese, and returned it to the grill. 'I'm just annoyed because there was no earthly reason why you couldn't have—have taken his order, that's all. Now, hurry up. This is almost ready.'

For the next half-hour, Samantha managed to keep herself too busy to pay any attention to her unwelcome visitor. There were meals to heat and serve, extra salads to be made, and plenty of dirty plates to load into the dishwasher. If Debbie thought she was less talkative than usual, she didn't say anything. Besides, she was busy too, and it wasn't until the café had practically cleared that Samantha noticed that *he* was still there.

It didn't really surprise her. She guessed Debbie would have said something if he had departed. But seeing him still seated at the table, apparently engrossed in a newspaper someone must have left behind, still infuriated her, and she wished she had the strength to throw him out.

'Go and tell him we're getting ready to close,' she murmured to Debbie, but the younger girl firmly shook her head.

'You know we don't close until half-past five,' she said. 'If you want to lie about it, you do it. He wasn't too pleased when I brought his sandwich, so don't expect me to do your dirty work.'

Samantha grimaced. 'I'm only asking you to fib a little. He doesn't know anything about this place.'

'How do you know that?'

Debbie was looking at her with that curious look again, and Samantha expelled a frustrated sigh. 'I don't—*know*—not for sure. But you haven't seen him round here before, have you? It's obvious he's not going to know what our hours are.'

'They're written on the door,' retorted Debbie flatly, and Samantha acknowledged that she had forgotten that.

'OK,' she said, giving in. 'I'll go and see if he's finished.'

He looked up as she reached the table, and, seeing who it was, he folded the newspaper and put it aside. 'Very nice,' he said, and for a moment she was so nervous, she didn't know what he was talking about. 'The sandwich,' he prompted, noticing her blank expression. 'As good as any I've tasted. You had the consistency of the cheese just right.'

Samantha allowed all the air to escape from her lungs, and then took a steadying breath. 'So,' she said, 'is that all? Would you like your bill?'

'What I'd like is for you to sit down with me,' he replied evenly, no trace of humour in his expression now. 'You've been running yourself ragged for the last hour, at least. Don't you think you deserve a break?'

'I'll have a break when all the customers have gone,' she told him crisply, wishing she had taken the time to go to the bathroom before marching over here. Her brown hair was coming loose from the single braid she had plaited that morning, and she was sure her face was streaked with sweat. It shouldn't matter how she looked as far as he was concerned, but it did. She couldn't help remembering Melissa Mainwaring's pale, exquisite face, and her long, elegant hand on his sleeve.

He shrugged then, and stood up, immediately putting her at even more of a disadvantage. In her low-heeled shoes, she was little more than five and a half feet, and she had to tilt her head to look up at him.

'What time do you close?' he asked, and Samantha, who had expected him to ask how much he owed her, took a step backwards.

'I—half-past five,' she said, recognising that there was
no point in lying about it. 'Um—that'll be two pounds
twenty. One-fifty for the sandwich, and seventy pence for
the juice.'

She hated asking him for the money. She would have
much preferred to say it was on the house. But Debbie
would want to know why she hadn't charged him, and it
was too complicated to go into details.

'What?' He frowned. And then, realising what she was
saying, he pulled a five pound note from the pocket of his
leather trousers. 'Here.' He handed it over. 'Now, will
you have a drink with me, *after* you close?'

Samantha was staggered. 'Why?'

He shrugged. 'Why not?'

'I can't.' Samantha shook her head.

'Why can't you?'

Samantha swallowed, and glanced behind her to make
sure Debbie wasn't eavesdropping on their conversation. Then, lifting her left hand, she showed him the diamond solitaire Paul had given her. 'I don't think my
fiancé would approve.'

He expelled his breath then, and there was a distinct
note of sarcasm in his harsh voice as he said, 'I'm only
asking you to have a drink with me. I'm not planning on
taking you to bed.'

Samantha's cheeks flamed. 'You wouldn't get the
chance!' she retorted hotly, despising the shiver of excitement that ran through her at his words. Had Melissa
Mainwaring been to bed with him? she wondered. Was
that why he had treated her with such a lack of respect?

'Perhaps not.' He was disturbingly equivocal about her
denial. 'So—will you join me for a drink? Anywhere you
like. You know the area better than I do.'

An image of sitting in some smoky bar, with him beside her on an intimate banquette, flashed into her mind. She could already feel the hard strength of his thigh, as it brushed against hers, and smell the heady warmth of his breath, as it cooled her hot temple . . .

With an effort, she thrust those thoughts aside, and struggled to appear indifferent. 'I can't,' she said again, smoothing the note he had given her between fingers that were slightly damp. 'I—er—I'll get your change.'

But when she closed the till he was gone. She was left with the two pounds eighty pence in her hand, feeling rather like a cheap tart who hadn't given satisfaction. It didn't help when Debbie came and looked over her shoulder either. 'Some tip,' she remarked, continuing on her way to clear the table. But Samantha felt like taking his money and throwing it into the street.

The afternoon dragged. Once the lunchtime rush was over, they were never very busy, catering mainly for young mothers with toddlers, or older women wanting a break in the middle of their shopping.

Debbie left at twenty-five past. Her bus was at twenty-five to six, and Samantha generally let her go in time to catch it. Otherwise, she felt obliged to drop the girl off on her way home, and that entailed a detour.

Samantha was seeing Paul that evening, so she worked fairly speedily after the 'Closed' sign had been put in place. They were going to the new multiplex cinema to see a film Paul had told her about. He was picking her up from home at a quarter-past seven. Which should give her time to have a shower, and hopefully dispel the feelings of ambivalance that had hung about her all afternoon.

She left the café at twenty to six, setting the safety alarm, and locking the door behind her. It was a cool

evening, with drops of rain in the air, and she hoped it
would warm up for Easter, which was only a couple of
weeks away. Although some sturdy cherry trees were attempting to come into blossom, the east wind was deter-
ring all but the hardiest growth. It was one of the chilliest
springs Samantha could remember, and she wrapped her
raincoat closely about her as she made a dash for her van.

The van coughed, but it started at the second attempt,
and she patted the wheel approvingly. The little Mini had
never let her down yet, but there was no denying she
needed a larger vehicle.

And yet, she argued frowningly, waiting for a break in
the traffic so that she could pull away, if she wasn't going to continue with her outside catering, was there a lot
of point? The Mini was quite capable of running her
around town, and she seldom went any distance in the
ordinary way unless she was with Paul.

Unwillingly, the reasons why she was having second
thoughts about the catering brought *that* man's face to
mind. She hadn't forgotten what had happened at
lunchtime. On the contrary, she was having the greatest
difficulty keeping thoughts of him at bay. The trouble
was, no matter how she might deny it to herself, she had
been curious as to why he had taken the trouble to come
and find her. And, although the idea that he might have
some personal interest in her was too far-fetched to contemplate, she felt a quiver of excitement whenever she
thought of him.

'Get real, Sam!' she chided herself angrily, as she
braked for the lights at Park Terrace. What possible interest could someone like him have in an ordinary female like herself? She wasn't chic; she wasn't elegant; she
wasn't even particularly good-looking. The only advantages she possessed were that she had fairly long legs for

a girl of her height, and that she was blessedly slim. Having said that, her breasts had always been a little too heavy, and her fine toffee hair had to be permed to give it any body. At present, it was in that crimped state of being neither straight nor curly, and for working she dragged it ruthlessly into a tight braid. Not exactly what he was used to, she was sure, even if he couldn't compete with the rich Prince Georgio.

She had guessed that that was why he hadn't arrived at the party like all the other guests. It was obvious he and Melissa Mainwaring knew one another rather better than her wealthy fiancé was aware. But she guessed Miss Mainwaring would always have an eye to the main chance. And she had chosen security, instead of...what? *Love*? Samantha's nose wrinkled. Lust, more like, she essayed scornfully, not liking where her musings were taking her. But she couldn't prevent the image of the pair of them on a bed together from invading her troubled thoughts, and the knowledge of how that made her feel was like a bitter taste in her mouth.

In consequence, she spent the evening trying to make it up to Paul. Not that he was aware of what she was doing. He just thought she was more affectionate than usual. Which made for a rather difficult scene, when it was time to say goodnight. He naturally assumed she would welcome his advances, and she was hot, and dispirited, when she eventually let herself into the house. Why couldn't she be like other girls? she wondered, wearily, as she tugged a brush through her tumbled hair. Of course, most of the girls she had gone to school with were married by now, so they didn't have this problem. Nevertheless, she remembered how they used to talk before they got a ring on their finger. And her reactions to Paul bore little resemblance to their eager confidences.

The phone rang soon after she got into work the next morning. And when she picked it up a voice she didn't recognise said, 'Miss Maxwell, please.'

'This is Miss Maxwell,' she replied, automatically reaching for her notebook. Her doubts of the evening before had been dispelled somewhat by the unexpected arrival of the sun, and she swiftly decided that if this was another catering assignment she would do it.

'I understand you operate an independent catering service,' the unfamiliar male voice continued, and Samantha dropped into the chair beside her desk. The tiny office was really just a storeroom, off the main serving area, but it did provide a little privacy, when the café was busy.

'That's right,' she said now. 'I have catered for a couple of dinner parties recently. What did you have in mind? Buffet catering is fairly standard, but more formal menus can be to your choice, of course.'

'Of course.' The man was silent for a moment, and Samantha wondered if he was having second thoughts. But then, he added, 'Perhaps it would be best if we could meet and discuss the arrangements. It is rather an important occasion, and I wouldn't like there to be any hitches.'

Samantha frowned. 'Would this dinner party be in London?' she asked, mentally cataloguing her plans for the rest of the week. Apart from being tied up during the day with the café, her evenings were reasonably flexible. As long as Paul didn't take offence if she had to cancel any of his arrangements.

'It's—er—it's a boardroom lunch actually,' said the man, after another moment's hesitation. 'Does that present any problems?'

'A lunch!' Samantha was dismayed. It hadn't occurred to her to consider that she might be invited to cater for a lunch. This was when she needed another assistant, she thought unhappily. There was no way Debbie could cope with the café single-handedly.

'It is in London,' added the man, as if to fill the void Samantha's procrastination had created. 'The company's J.P. Software International. The offices are just off the north side of Regent Street. You'd be catering for—approximately thirty people.'

'Yes.'

Samantha's brain was working madly. Despite what she had thought the night before, the idea of finding a lunchtime clientele was appealing. It had so many advantages. Not least, leaving her evenings free for other things. But, if she turned this down, she might not be asked again. She wondered how he had got her name. She really would have to get some cards printed.

'Well, Mr—er—er——?'

'Burgess,' supplied the man, after another of those infinitesimal pauses, but Samantha scarcely noticed.

'Well, Mr Burgess,' she said, 'I have to tell you, my previous experience has all been in evening engagements.'

All? She grimaced, and shifted the phone to her other ear. Two dinner parties didn't actually justify the word 'all'. But so what? She had to start somewhere.

'Does this mean you're not equipped to take on any afternoon appointments?' he queried, and Samantha sighed.

'Not exactly, no. But——'

'I suggest you come and talk it over with our PR department,' declared the man, overriding her objections. 'I'm sure we can work something out.'

Can we? For a moment, Samantha was half afraid she had said those words aloud, but there was no response from Mr Burgess, so she concluded, with some relief, that she hadn't. All the same, she didn't see how it could be done—unless her mother could be persuaded to help her.

'How—er—how did you get this number?' she asked, to give herself time to consider, and the man sucked in his breath.

'I—why, from a friend who attended a reception recently in Eyton Gate,' he replied swiftly, and, although Samantha was too absorbed to notice any inflexion in his voice, any connection with that occasion was enough to give her pause.

'Do you mind telling me who it was who gave you my number?' she enquired, realising it was hardly her business, but needing to know just the same.

'Um—no.' The man hesitated again, but Samantha was too anxious to hear what he had to say to notice. 'A chap by the name of Matthew Putnam,' he said offhandedly. And then, 'Does it matter? Is he a friend of yours, or something?'

CHAPTER FOUR

'THAT was a clever touch, Victor,' remarked Matthew, as his manservant put down the phone. His lips twisted admiringly. 'Implying that I might have some ulterior motive for recommending her was masterly. She was so busy denying any connection between us, she hardly noticed what she was agreeing to.'

'Well, I don't like it, Mr Putnam,' replied the older man tersely. 'For heaven's sake, why would you want to get involved with some second-rate waitress from Northfleet?'

Matthew's mouth tightened, and he swung the feet he had had propped on the edge of his desk, while Victor made the call to Samantha Maxwell, to the floor. 'She's not second-rate, and she's not a waitress,' he declared, his eyes cold as they surveyed the other man. 'And I'll—get involved, as you put it—with who I like. You may not think so, but you're not my keeper! Now, get out of here.'

'Yes, sir.'

Victor went, but Matthew could tell by the stiffness of the man's shoulders that he hadn't heard the last of it. He knew Victor too well, and Victor knew him. They'd been together too many years now for any minor contretemps to come between them. But, nevertheless, he was getting too familiar where Matthew's personal life was concerned. And, although he had never really liked Melissa, he had resigned himself to the fact that their relationship might become permanent.

But it hadn't, thought Matthew grimly, remembering the night of the engagement party with some distaste. And he had been fool enough to go there. If he'd had any sense he'd have stayed away, instead of believing he could beat Melissa at her own game.

Yet, to a point, he had, he conceded broodingly, remembering how outraged she'd been at finding him with the Maxwell girl. Melissa hadn't liked seeing him with another woman, however innocent that encounter had been.

But, after the girl had gone, it hadn't been so easy to play it cool. Melissa had got the wrong idea about him being there, in spite of the unconventional means of his arrival. And perhaps she had hoped he had had a change of heart. Whatever, she had certainly not acted like a woman who was engaged to another man. And he was only human, however degenerate that might make him feel.

He was glad now he had been the one to suggest they ought to go upstairs to the party. Playing games was one thing; deliberately seducing another man's fiancée was another. Which was probably why Melissa had made such a big thing of going to Ivanov, and hanging on his arm for the rest of the evening. She had wanted to make him squirm, and to a certain extent she had succeeded.

But he hadn't let her have it all her own way. Partly to provoke Melissa, and partly to relieve his own frustration, he had made a play for Briony Clarke, the second most attractive woman at the party—and one of Melissa's closest friends.

The irony was, Briony had fallen for it, hook, line and sinker. And, when she did, Matthew had discovered it wasn't as much fun hurting people as he had thought. In consequence, he had stalked out long before the party was over, uncaring what interpretation Melissa might put on his actions.

But, curiously enough, it hadn't been Melissa or Briony who had occupied his thoughts when he eventually got to bed. He had found himself thinking about the Maxwell girl, and remembering how terrified she had been, confronting him with a knife. God! A short laugh escaped him. She had really thought he was an intruder. But, designer stubble and all, he probably hadn't looked particularly civilised.

Nevertheless, it had been a novelty, being regarded as someone outside the law. Despite the fact that he had always fought for his independence, there had never been a time when he had actually broken the law. Oh, he had done things when he was a student that his mother and his grandfather would not have approved of, but they had had no criminal intent. Consequently, to be treated as a possible burglar or worse had had a singular appeal. Not that he wished to repeat it. The experience had been rather too real for comfort. But the girl—what was it her waitress had called her? Sam? Samantha—she had had definite possibilities.

Which was why he had made it his business to find out who, and what, she was. It hadn't been difficult Ivanov's secretary had been quite flattered that Matthew had been so impressed with the buffet that he wanted the number of the caterer. Lederer knew nothing of his previous association with Melissa, and even less about Samantha Maxwell.

In truth, Matthew didn't know what he intended when he drove down to Northfleet, a couple of days later. Maybe Victor had a point. Maybe it was the fact that she came from a different background from his that had excited his interest. Certainly she was nothing like the women he was used to dealing with. It wasn't just that she worked for her living. Many of the women he knew ran galleries, or boutiques, or were involved in public relations and modelling. One or two of them even owned their own businesses, though nothing quite so physical as running a café. No, it was more to do with her attitude; with the kind of defensive stance she had adopted towards him. She didn't seem to like him, which was also a novelty, for, although he had never seen any great attraction in his appearance, the fact remained that most women seemed to find him presentable.

Even so, it was hard to justify what he was doing now, even to himself. He didn't honestly know why he was doing it. Just because she had turned him down, he had engineered this totally trumped-up charade. And why? So she would accept an invitation to see him again. Only she didn't think she was seeing him. Her appointment was supposedly with Andy Lucas, his public relations manager.

His jaw hardening, Matthew pulled the computer keyboard towards him and punched in the code for the current system he was working on. But even when the complicated program unfolded on the screen he found no escape in the data it provided. His mind was still active with thoughts of the upcoming meeting with Samantha Maxwell, and despite his impatience he was tempted to cancel it.

Still in two minds, he switched off the computer and left his study. He had decided to go into the office after all, and he would think about what he was going to do about the Maxwell girl later. It wasn't that important, for

Pete's sake! She was only a blasted waitress! She ought to be flattered he was taking an interest in her!

But, as he changed out of the sweat-suit he had worn to the gym earlier, he knew he was being less than fair. He might never have been involved with a woman like her before, but, conversely, he had never treated any woman differently from another. He wasn't a snob, and he certainly didn't consider himself better than anyone else because of his background. Which was why trying to find excuses for what he was doing this time was proving so difficult. What did he want from her? Companionship? *Sex*? For pity's sake, could he be that desperate?

And yet, as he pulled on navy blue trousers and rummaged through a pile of silk shirts for one he liked, he was uncomfortably aware of the hardening in his groin when he recalled how good her breasts had felt, cushioned against his chest. She had had rather full breasts, he remembered, and long, long legs. Her face hadn't been particularly striking; her cheeks had been too round, and her mouth too big. But it had been a sexy mouth, particularly when she had been frightened, and her lower lip had jutted forwards. And she had beautiful green eyes, long, and slightly slanted, and fringed by dark lashes, which must surely be cosmetic.

His lips twisted. For someone who denied a serious interest in the girl, he certainly remembered a lot about her. Remembered, too, a distinct unwillingness to let her go, even when Melissa had come down the stairs and found them. But that had probably been because he knew how sucked Melissa would feel, seeing them together. That was probably why he was pursuing the connection. Because he knew how infuriated Melissa would be.

His friend and managing director Robert Prescott was deep in a discussion about computer viruses with their

sales manager Martin Ryan when Matthew arrived at the
office. J.P. Software International occupied the top two
floors of a high-rise in Cumberland Place, with Matthew's office, and the boardroom, and the offices of his
senior management team, on the upper level. Now, Matthew came to rest his shoulder against the frame of Robert's door, acknowledging his second-in-command's
raised eyebrows with a grimace of his own.

'I know,' he said. 'You didn't expect to see me. Well, I
thought it was time I came to see what you were doing.'

Robert grinned, their relationship one of long standing, and of mutual respect. 'I'm glad to see you're still
alive,' he remarked, as Martin Ryan got up from the desk
and made some comment about having things to do. He
waited until the door had closed behind the other man
before adding drily, 'According to your mother, you're
drinking yourself to death!'

'Mmm.' Matthew flung himself into the chair across
from his friend and pulled a face. 'My mother exagger-
ates,' he declared, leaning forward to pluck a brochure
advertising some sophisticated hardware from Robert's desk. 'What's this stuff like?' he queried, flicking
through its pages. 'I hear these new lap-tops weigh less
than six pounds.'

Robert regarded him tolerantly. 'So I hear,' he conceded, prepared to wait until Matthew chose to tell him
why he had really come into the office. It wasn't just to
exchange gossip. Matthew wasn't like that.

'Of course, they're still working on the screens.'

'Yes.'

'And I guess only the most expensive of them have
anything like the capability of a desktop.'

'Yes.'

Matthew looked up, aware of the monosyllabic answers he was receiving, and the reason for them. He gave a rueful grin. 'I'm so glad you agree.'

Robert shrugged. 'What's not to agree? We get a dozen of those pamphlets dropped through our door every day. They all claim to have made a breakthrough in computer technology. Some of them have. Most of them haven't. They've just adapted someone else's idea.'

Matthew tossed the brochure back on to the desk. 'So speaks the complete cynic.'

'You get cynical in this business,' retorted Robert, his hand hovering over the button on his intercom. 'Can I interest you in some coffee?'

Matthew shrugged. 'Why not? What's a little caffeine between friends?'

Robert spoke to his secretary, and then lay back in his chair, steepling his fingers. 'So,' he said, curiosity getting the better of him, 'did you finish the program? Is that what we owe the honour of this visit to?'

Matthew arched one dark brow. 'Don't be facetious, Rob. It doesn't suit you. Until recently, I spent as much time in this office as you did.'

'Yeah.' Robert had to acknowledge that this was true. 'I guess you must have decided to take your mother's advice for once.'

'My mother's advice is to leave the running of this place to you, and go and live in Athens,' retorted Matthew grimly. 'What's your opinion of that?'

Robert frowned. 'You know what my opinion is. I'm an administrator, Matt. You're the brains around here.'

'I'd dispute that,' said Matthew flatly, breaking off as a knock sounded at the door. He waited until Robert's secretary had set the tray containing their cups of coffee on the desk and left the room before continuing, 'But what will happen when my grandfather retires is anybody's guess.'

Robert grimaced. 'Well, let's hope that day is a long way off,' he declared firmly. 'Now——' He handed one of the cups to his friend. 'Sugar but no cream, is that right?'

'Thanks.' Matthew took the cup, and gave a cursory glance at its contents. 'Black as hell's kettle. Just as I like it.'

Robert's lips twitched. 'OK.' He paused. 'So why did you decide to come in today? Is there a problem?'

'You might say that.' Matthew swallowed a mouthful of the coffee, and scowled as it scalded his throat. 'Damn! This is hot as hell, too! What's Judy trying to do? Burn my tongue out?'

'Hardly.' Robert was cautious as he sipped from his own cup. 'She was probably hoping you'd like it hot! Or that's the rumour anyway.'

'Ha, ha!' Matthew regarded his friend without rancour. 'But, as it happens, I do have a problem. A slight one, anyway. And—well, I want your help.'

Robert put down his cup. 'Go on.'

Matthew sighed. 'It's not that easy.'

'Why?' Robert looked wary. 'Is it personal?'

Matthew took a breath. 'Yes.'

Robert looked resigned. 'Don't tell me: you've seen Melissa.'

'I have seen Melissa.' Matthew's expression hardened. 'But that's not why I'm here.'

'No?'

'No.' Matthew was sardonic. 'As a matter of fact, it's someone else.'

'Another woman?' Robert looked staggered now.

'Yes.' Matthew half wished he hadn't started this. 'I met her at Melissa's engagement party.'

'*You* went to Melissa's engagement party?'

'I was invited,' agreed Matthew flatly. 'So what? We're still civilised human beings, aren't we?'

Robert shook his head. 'You tell me!'

'What's that supposed to mean?'

'Well, you haven't been particularly civil since Melissa walked out, have you?' he protested, reacting to Matthew's angry response.

'Maybe not.' Matthew took a moment to acknowledge the truth of that. 'Anyway, I'm going to have to live with it, aren't I? One way or the other.'

'So what's your problem?' Robert was curious. 'Who is this girl, anyway? Do I know her?'

'Unlikely.' Matthew's mouth flattened. 'Her name's Maxwell. Samantha Maxwell.'

'Does she live in London?'

'No.' Matthew shook his head. 'She lives in a little town in Essex. She's just a nice girl from a very ordinary background.'

'You're kidding!'

'No, I'm not.' Matthew was trying his best not to let Robert rile him in this. 'Anyway, who she is isn't important. What she does is.'

'Come again.'

Matthew changed tack. 'Do you remember telling me about this proposed meeting we're having with Koysaki?'

'I should do. I arranged it.'

'That's right.' Matthew paused. 'Well, I wondered if it might be a good idea to throw a lunch for them here. In the boardroom. I know you were talking about taking them out for dinner, but it occurred to me that a working lunch might suit all of us better.'

Robert blinked. 'OK. If you say so.' He lifted his shoulders. 'Forgive me, but what does this have to do with your new girlfriend?'

'She's not my new girlfriend,' declared Matthew drily. 'I don't even think she likes me. But——' he expelled his breath '—she's a professional caterer. And, I've pre-empted your approval, and asked her if she could give us a quote.'

'For the Koysaki lunch?'

'Yep.'

Robert shook his head. 'Are you telling me this is the only way you can see her again?'

'Something like that.'

'Does she know who you are?'

'No.'

'Then tell her.'

'No.' Matthew got up from his chair, and paced over to the window. 'If you knew her, you wouldn't even suggest it. Besides which, she's engaged.'

'God, Matt!' Robert finished his coffee, and thrust his cup aside. 'What is all this about? I don't believe you're that desperate to see this girl again! And, at the risk of getting my head bitten off, what about Melissa?'

'What about Melissa?' Matthew pushed his hands into his trouser pockets. 'I must say, for someone who professes to care about me, you certainly like turning the knife.'

'Don't be stupid!' Robert pushed back his chair, and got to his feet. 'It's just that—well, a week ago you weren't even returning my calls. Now, you've come up with this idea of getting some girl to arrange a lunch for the Japanese. Do I take it she was the caterer at Melissa's party?'

'It was Ivanov's party, actually,' said Matthew, splitting hairs. 'But yes. She did organise it. And it was pretty good, too. I think you'll be impressed.'

Robert looked nonplussed. 'I can't believe this, you know. Is she a raving beauty, or what?'

'No.' Matthew had to be honest. 'As I say, she's fairly ordinary, really. She has nice eyes, and nice——' he shunned the word *breasts* and added '—legs. She—intrigues me.'

'Because she turned you down, probably,' remarked Robert drily. 'Honestly, Matt, are you sure you know what you're doing?'

'No.' Matthew gave a rueful grin, and Robert couldn't help responding. 'But Melissa's going to be mad as hell when she finds out!'

Matthew's personal assistant paused in her boss's doorway and gave her employer a puzzled look. 'I say what?'

'You just tell her that Mr Burgess isn't here, but that his second-in-command will see her. OK?'

Mrs Mackay sighed. 'But who is Mr Burgess, Mr Putnam?' Her stalwart Scottish nature rebelled at the deception. 'What if she asks me that?'

'She won't.' Matthew tipped his chair back on its rear castors. 'Just do it, Mary, there's a good girl. Oh—and bring me the Koysaki file.'

Mrs Mackay returned a few moments later with the requested item, but her homely face still wore a look of disapproval. However, having worked for Matthew for the past eight years, she was reluctantly prepared to do as he asked. In every other way, he was a considerate employer, and she never stopped thanking her lucky stars that, at the age of forty-two, she had landed such a plum position. Oh, she knew why. It was common knowledge in the office that Matthew had grown tired of younger, more glamorous PAs, whose prime objective had been to marry the boss. Nevertheless, she considered herself extremely fortunate to enjoy his confidence, even if, in this instance, he had chosen not to be absolutely frank.

The door closed behind her, and Matthew flipped open the Koysaki file. The Japanese company, whose representatives were flying to England at the end of the week, were looking for a software company through which they could channel their own product into Europe. It was a deal that interested Matthew greatly, offering as it did the opportunities for a similar expansion of J.P. Software into Japan. And, although he usually left all the talking to Robert, this was one occasion when he wouldn't mind sitting in on their discussions.

But, in spite of his interest in the project, Matthew found he couldn't concentrate. Instead, he closed the file again, and tapped his fingernails against the cardboard folder. What if she didn't come? he thought tautly, remembering how offhand she had been when he'd seen her. What if she'd discovered that Victor had nothing to do with J.P. Software International? Or—conversely— that Matthew Putnam had? It would be just his bad luck if she'd chosen to check out her client. And, in spite of her indifference, he didn't think she'd forgotten his name.

The buzzer on his desk sounded, and he started at the sound. Damn, he thought, he was as edgy as a roadrunner. Thank God Mrs Mackay couldn't see him.

'Yes,' he said, finding his voice, and depressing the receiver. 'What is it?'

'Miss Maxwell is here, Mr—er——' Matthew winced as she stuttered over the omission. 'Um—shall I send her in?'

'If you would.' Matthew took a deep breath and rose to his feet, no longer so convinced that this was a good idea.

Mrs Mackay opened the door. 'Miss Maxwell, sir,' she said, carefully avoiding a repeat of her earlier hesitation. She ushered the younger woman forward. 'Would you like some coffee?'

'Why not?'

Matthew said the words without giving them a great deal of thought. His attention was all on the newcomer, his eyes narrowing over slightly windswept curls and a pale grey suit whose skirt ended a couple of inches above her knee. She looked the same, but different, a harassed efficiency giving way to nervous anticipation.

That is, until she saw him; until she recognised that she had been tricked. Then, she glanced round at the departing Mrs Mackay with a distinct air of uncertainty, her hitherto pale features deepening with attractive colour. And she was attractive, Matthew admitted reluctantly. More attractive than he had been prepared to acknowledge. Those wide green eyes possessed a timeless beauty, although at present their expression was anything but remote.

'You,' she said, in an accusing tone, as the door closed behind Mrs Mackay. 'You're not Mr Burgess!'

Matthew forwent the idea of offering her his hand, and gestured to the chair at the other side of the desk. 'Did anyone say I was?' he queried, arching one dark brow. 'Allow me to introduce myself: I'm Matthew Putnam.'

'I know that.' Her lips tightened.

'Very well. Won't you sit down?' he suggested. 'The coffee won't be long.'

'I don't want any coffee,' she retorted tensely, gripping the leather portfolio she had brought with her, with both hands. Her tongue appeared to wet lips that were a delicious shade of copper, and Matthew found his eyes following its provocative progress. 'Just tell me why you've brought me here. And wasted a whole morning of my time!'

Matthew felt a twinge of anger. Just who the hell did she think she was? he wondered hotly. As far as she knew, she had been brought here to discuss a business proposition. What had he said to give her the impression that anything had changed?

'I suggest you sit down—and cool down,' he advised, keeping his own tone as unemotional as he could manage. 'Or is this the usual way you conduct business? I have to tell you, I've not come across these confrontational tactics before.'

She took a few deep breaths, and the sides of her jacket parted and came together invitingly. She was wearing a cream blouse under her jacket, and the lacy jabot at its neck fluttered accordingly. Her shoulders were back, and the rounded curve of her breasts swelled against the soft material. Matthew felt his own unwilling response to her undoubted femininity, and subsided into his chair. To hell with being polite, he decided grimly. Self-respect was more important just at present.

But, as if his words had aroused some doubt in her mind, too, Miss Maxwell chose that moment to inch forward, and brace her hips on the edge of the chair opposite. Matthew wouldn't have said she was sitting exactly, although she had drawn her knees tightly together. Nevertheless, she was not looking down at him, as she would have been otherwise, and her grip on the portfolio was less tense.

Her eyes flickered up, met his, and flickered away again. Eyes that had hazel flecks in them now, turning the green to grey. He watched as she cast a surreptitious glance about the room, before returning her attention to the portfolio.

'I—do I take it there really is a business lunch to cater for?' she asked at last, and Matthew knew a momentary sense of self-contempt. It was so easy to manipulate her, he thought disgustedly, tempted to lay bare the whole charade. But on the heels of this thought came the memory of how Melissa had treated him, and he consoled himself with the knowledge that she could have refused the invitation.

'Naturally, there's a lunch,' he said now, managing to sound convincingly put out. 'As— as my colleague said over the phone, it's for approximately twenty-five to thirty people. Our guests are Japanese, actually. So perhaps you could include some ethnic food as well.'

'Japanese?' Her eyes widened as they turned to his, and Matthew had the crazy thought that he might drown in their depths. His fingers itched to touch the long silky lashes that curled back against her lids, and smooth the curve of her temple, where it disappeared into the streaky mass of hair. 'I'm afraid I know nothing about Japanese food.'

'No?'

Matthew held her gaze deliberately, and saw the moment when panic entered her eyes. For seconds longer, she allowed him to mesmerise her, as a snake would hypnotise a rabbit. Then Mrs Mackay knocked at the door, and the compelling mood was broken.

'Just put the tray over there,' Matthew ordered, making space for it on his desk, his tone betraying just a trace of the irritation he was feeling. But Mrs Mackay noticed it, and her face assumed a matching expression.

'Can I get you anything else, Mr Putnam?' she enquired, and Matthew could hear the increased Scottish twang in her tone, which denoted her disapproval.

'No, thanks,' he said, impatient for her to leave them alone, and she took the hint.

'Well, I'll just be outside, if you want me,' she added, as a parting shot, and Matthew guessed that was as much for Miss Maxwell's benefit as his own.

With the door closed, he decided to take advantage of the opportunity the coffee afforded. 'Won't you join me?' he requested of her now bent head and, although she was clearly unwilling, discretion fought with valour, and won.

'Thank you,' she said, though he noticed she didn't trust herself to meet his gaze again. 'Um—milk, and no sugar.'

'It's cream,' he said wryly, and she pulled a rueful face.

'Another nail in the diet,' she quipped, giving the first indication that she was beginning to trust him. She took the cup he handed her, but avoided touching his hand. 'Thanks.' She sipped, and looked around her. 'This is a beautiful office.'

'I'm glad you like it.' Matthew poured himself a cup of coffee, but made no attempt to drink it. Instead, he lay back in his chair and said, 'So—who's minding the café today?'

It was a mistake. She stiffened at once, and he knew she was remembering his invasion of her space. But what the hell; for all she knew he had been down there, checking out the place. Not for any *personal* reasons.

'Is it important?' she asked now, and once again those cool eyes were turned on him. Evidently, anger provided a defence behind which she could shelter. But he wasn't daunted by such a puerile display.

'Not at all,' he countered, pushing himself forward, and resting his elbows on the desk. 'Are you usually this touchy with would-be clients?'

A deepening trace of warm colour entered her neck, just below the jawline, and spread rapidly upwards. 'I'm sorry,' she said tightly, setting her cup back on the tray with a betraying clatter. 'As a matter of fact, this whole—catering—thing is a new departure for me, and I'm not at all sure I want to continue with it.' She gathered up the leather case that had been resting on her knees, holding it in front of her like a would-be shield, and got to her feet. 'I—appreciate your confidence, but I don't think I'm the person to—to—accommodate you in this matter. I don't have the experience, and—and I certainly don't feel it would be—appropriate for me to—to waste your time and mine in—in continuing with this discussion.' She sidestepped the chair, and began to retreat towards the door. 'I'm sure you'll find—someone else——'

Her excuses ended abruptly as Matthew left his chair and came after her. Impatience marred his lean dark features as he strode past her, successfully blocking her exit and bringing her to a standstill.

'You *appreciate*, that you can't *accommodate*, and it wouldn't be *appropriate*,' he mocked harshly, realising that if he wasn't careful she was going to walk out of here without leaving him even the flimsiest of excuses for seeing her again. His lips twisted. 'What's the matter, Miss Maxwell? Are you afraid of me?'

'No!'

The denial was swift enough, but hardly convincing. Her hands were white-knuckled as they gripped the portfolio. But, although he was sure she would have liked

to keep a healthy distance between them, courage, or
simply grim determination, kept her where she was.

'No?' he echoed scornfully, giving up all hope of handling this calmly. The scent of her body was drifting to
his nostrils, a mixture of skin cream, and cologne, and a
definite trace of nervous arousal. Whatever she said, he
did disturb her, and the urge to touch her was growing
out of control.

'Will you get out of my way?' she asked tensely, evidently still believing she could handle the situation. And
he supposed she could, if she chose to cry for help, and
Mrs Mackay came rushing to the rescue.

'Will you tell me why you've changed your mind about
organising the lunch?' he countered, and, unable to prevent himself, he put out a hand and tucked a silky coil of
hair behind her ear. Her head jerked away from his fingers, but she didn't dash his hand away. And, acting
purely on impulse, he allowed the tips of his fingers to
trail away down her neck to the collarless jacket of her
suit.

'I should have thought that was obvious,' she declared now, rushing into speech, as if it was the only way
she could cope with his advances. 'You don't want my
professional services, Mr Putnam. You just want to play
sexual games! Well, I'm sorry, but I'm not interested in
your offer, whatever it is. So step out of the way, and let
me go.'

Matthew's jaw hardened. Until she spoke, he had
thought he might have let her go, unchallenged. He knew
she was engaged. She had displayed her ring proudly.
And, despite his suspicions, he had been having second
thoughts about his intentions. He had actually felt a
twinge of remorse for setting her up this way. She was a
decent girl, after all, and if he needed a scapegoat there

were plenty of other women around. Women who had nothing to lose.

But his finer feelings foundered on the sharp edge of her contempt. It was one thing for him to think about letting her off the hook, and quite another for her to believe she could force the issue. For God's sake, didn't she know better than to throw her indifference in his face? Didn't she know how irresistible it was to prove her wrong?

His eyes moved over her, noticing that for all her brave outburst she was breathing rather fast. The lace jabot fairly quivered as she fought to calm herself, and he guessed that only her grip on the portfolio prevented her from making some nervous gesture.

She was biting her lips, too, a sure sign that she was agitated. The lower lip was red and sore from being drawn between her teeth, and her tongue came to soothe it, before it was attacked again.

'Don't you ever play games, Sam?' he asked softly, and saw the start she gave at his casual use of her name. Perhaps she'd assumed he didn't know it. After all, she hadn't heard his conversation with her waitress.

'I—can I leave?' she demanded, instead of answering him. Her voice had risen slightly, and he guessed that she was anxious. Anxious, and a little apprehensive, he guessed shrewdly. What would she do if he said no?

'Why don't you just sit down and we'll talk about it?' he said, tracing the edge of her jacket with his thumb and foretinger. Even now, her vulnerability pricked his conscience. But, when the backs of his fingers brushed the curve of her breast, the feeling was electric. Warm skin, lightly covered by the fine fabric of her blouse, swelled against his hand, and the need to feel their fullness overpowered him.

But before his fingers could explore those tantalising peaks, she had dashed his hand away and darted for the door. Only an instinctive lunge on his part prevented her from snatching the door open, and his palm slammed into the panel, right beside her head.

She spun round against the door, her eyes showing her dismay. No, not dismay; that was too mild a term. She looked shocked; astounded; desperate to escape, and— hunted. Yes, that was the word. She looked like a cornered animal. And, in spite of his intentions, Matthew knew a moment's regret.

'Are you mad?' she choked, as his other hand came to rest on the other side of her head, effectively imprisoning her against the door. 'I—I'll scream!'

'Go ahead,' he said recklessly, the feminine scent of her body enveloping him once more. The more she fought him, the more aroused she became, and he didn't believe she would call for help and humiliate herself so completely.

But he was wrong. He apprehended the fact just a split second before she opened her mouth. And, although it wasn't the way he had intended to play it, there was only one way to silence her. With a muffled oath, he cut the scream off at its source, his mouth fastening over hers with bruising insistence.

She resisted, of course. The leather portfolio went flying, and she used both hands to try and force him away. Her balled fists slammed into his stomach, making him catch his breath. But it was when her knee attempted to connect with the most vulnerable part of his body that he reacted more forcefully, lowering his weight against her, and pinning her against the door.

Her jaw sagged, stunned by the crushing pressure of his heavy frame. He was robbing her of breath, he knew, but it was the only way to control her, and his hand left the door to curl about her throat. He stroked the taut skin, caressing and soothing, and when he felt her strength ebbing he slid his tongue between her teeth.

She bit it, but not hard, and beneath his insistence the tenor of the kiss changed. Her mouth softened under his, her lips opening of their own free will, to admit his searching invasion. Her hands, stilled by his brutal subjugation, now clutched the lapels of his jacket, as if needing a lifeline, and her legs parted helplessly when he wedged his thigh between.

She was so soft, so submissive; silk, and lace, and sweetness, tongue and lips yielding to the mastery of his. She was trembling; he could feel it; but fire leapt between them as he continued to possess her mouth. His body was responding; getting heavier; hardening; making him wish he could take her there, hard against the door. Or maybe on the floor; his senses reeled at the prospect. Lifting her legs, wrapping them around him, plunging deep into her hot, damp core...

He should have realised it had been too easy. Her sudden weakness; her submission. He should have suspected there was more to it than sex.

But the truth was, he was too bemused by his own arousal to give any thought to what she might be thinking, might be feeling. He was seduced by the idea of what it would be like, undressing her, making love with her, showing her how perfectly they could fit together. He felt so sure of her response that he was foolish enough to ease away from her, so that he could separate her blouse from the waistband of her skirt. He wanted to slide his hands underneath the filmy fabric. The prospect of touching her soft skin tantalised him, and the button-hard nipples were just aching for his caress.

Or so he had fondly imagined. But, once again, he should have known better than to think he could anticipate anything she might do. She must have just been waiting for some show of weakness on his part, and when he drew away from her she took her chance.

Afterwards, Matthew realised, she had only succeeded because he'd let her. If he had been on his guard, she would never have been able to push him off balance. But he wasn't, and she did, and he was still reeling against a potted palm when she fled out of the door. He heard Mrs Mackay utter a startled cry as a waste-paper bin was overturned, but the slamming of the outer door revealed she hadn't faltered. Which left him with the ignominious task of explaining to his assistant why Miss Maxwell had left in such a hurry and tamping down his own frustration at the inept way he had handled the situation.

CHAPTER FIVE

'BUT I don't understand. Why haven't you reported it to the police?'

'Because I haven't.' Samantha's head was aching, and she wished her mother would stop looking at her as if *she* had done something dreadful. 'It's only a leather portfolio, Mum. Nothing to get steamed up about.'

'I shouldn't have to remind you that your dad and I bought you that portfolio,' retorted her mother shortly. 'And you say you dropped it on the Tube, and you haven't even mentioned it to the authorities!'

Samantha took off her suit jacket, and draped it over a chair. 'I've told you: I didn't realise it was missing until I was walking up from the station.' She glanced round the café, which was empty except for a couple of teenagers, sitting at the table in the window. 'Anyway, thanks for covering for me. Has it been busy?'

'It was busy at lunchtime.' Mrs Maxwell was offhand 'I must say, I thought you'd have been back before this. It's nearly five!'

'I know. I'm sorry.' Samantha had prepared herself for this while she was tramping round the streets of London. 'But you know what it's like. The buses are all full, and you can't get a taxi.'

'For three hours!' Mrs Maxwell wasn't convinced. 'I expected you back about two o'clock. Three, at the latest. What on earth have you been doing all this time? Did you arrange the booking?'

'Well—no.' Samantha knew there was no point in pretending otherwise. Her mother would find out soon enough. 'I—they wanted an ethnic meal. Japanese food; sushi, stuff like that. I couldn't do it.'

Mrs Maxwell stared at her. 'And didn't they tell you that when they arranged the interview?'

'Obviously not.' But Samantha could feel the colour invading her cheeks as she spoke. God, how she hated all this subterfuge! She was no good at lying. No good at anything, except getting herself into trouble.

Her mother sniffed. 'And it took you six hours to find that out?'

'The journey took the better part of three hours,' protested Samantha, able to be honest about that, at least. 'You know what the traffic is like in town. That's why I didn't take the car.'

'Even so...'

'Well——' Samantha licked her lips, and discovered they were still bare of lipstick. Damn, she should have found time to renew her make-up. But she had been walking around in a daze ever since she left Matthew Putnam's office. And it had taken her some time to find out where she was. 'I had to wait,' she offered feebly. 'And then we had coffee, and talked about—about other things.'

'What other things?'

'This and that.' Samantha shrugged, and jabbed a button on the till, pretending to be examining the takings. 'Just—just the usual sort of things, Mum. How cold it's been. How pretty the blossom is in the park. What sort of summer we're going to have.'

'Huh.' Her mother still sounded sceptical. 'It seems to me you've just been wasting your time. And mine, too, I might add. Well, I hope this isn't going to happen too often.'

'It won't.' Samantha closed the till with a snap that brought Debbie out of the small office, ostensibly to see what was going on. But Samantha didn't doubt she had heard everything that had been said. There was no privacy in the café.

Mrs Maxwell arched her sandy brows now. 'No?'

'No,' said Samantha, giving Debbie a look that revealed she knew exactly what the girl had been doing. 'I've decided not to continue with the outside catering. As you said, Mum, I don't have the experience, or the expertise.'

Her mother looked surprised. 'But—I thought—don't you already have some bookings?'

'I have one,' agreed Samantha heavily, realising she was going to have to take some aspirin. Her head was really thumping now. 'A formal dinner on Saturday night. It was someone who attended Jenny's dinner party, and got my number from her. But after that I'm not accepting any more bookings. It's too—time-consuming. And I don't think I want the responsibility.'

Paul was delighted when he found out, and Mrs Maxwell couldn't wait to tell him. When he called round at the house later that evening, he had hardly got his coat off before she had spilled the news. Samantha, still nursing her headache, was in no mood to cope with his instant jubilation. She shouldn't have made that announcement, she thought wearily. She should have just stopped accepting bookings, and let them find out for themselves. Instead, she had to listen to Paul and her mother congratulating each other on knowing better all along. And pretend that she was happy, when what she really felt was sick.

Still, the combined effects of their delight and her headache did give her an excuse to say little in her own defence. And it also enabled her to refuse Paul's invitation to go for a drink at the pub, without arousing any animosity. She wanted to be alone with him, she told herself. Of course she did. But right now she felt too ashamed of what had happened earlier in the day to enjoy Paul's unalloyed affection. She felt as if she had betrayed him, and herself, and it would take some time to reconcile her actions.

The trouble was, she couldn't get what had happened out of her mind. Which wasn't surprising, really, she decided firmly. After all, women often required counselling after suffering an attempted rape. Only it hadn't been an attempted rape, she amended ruefully. An assault? Yes, definitely an assault. But she hadn't been in any real danger. Not of losing her virginity, or anything catastrophic like that. Dear God, if he had suspected she was still a virgin, he probably wouldn't have touched her with a barge-pole. That he hadn't was probably her bad luck.

Probably?

Her nails curled into her palms. That was the trouble. She was too ambivalent about the whole affair. And it was her response to what he had done that disturbed her most. Oh, she had consoled herself with the knowledge that, as soon as he had given her half a chance, she had been out of there. She had flown out of that office as if half the demons in hell had been at her heels. Goodness knew what his secretary must have thought. Overturning the waste-bin like that, and not even stopping to say sorry. So much for her role as a female executive. When it came right down to it, she had made a pig's ear out of the whole thing.

She sighed. It was no use. She could dodge about the issue as much as she liked, but when it came down to basics it was what had happened before she had made such an ignominious retreat that was causing her so much heartache. Even now, hours after the event, she could still feel the imprint of his body against hers, still taste the sensual invasion of his tongue. She had taken a shower earlier, and afterwards she had stood in front of her dressing-table mirror, wondering why she suddenly felt such an awareness of her own sexuality. Paul had never made her feel that way, and until now she had assumed it was something that came from knowing someone else completely; knowing as in the Biblical sense of the word, that was. But it wasn't true. When she had kissed Matthew Putnam—and in spite of her initial resistance that was what she had done— she had felt a kind of sliding abandonment; and the flame that had leapt between them had left no room for second thoughts. She had found herself in the totally unfamiliar position of wanting him to go on, of wanting him to touch her, and caress her, and do all those things she had always stopped Paul from doing. Dear God, with his mouth on hers she had been helpless, at the mercy of every mindless hunger in her body. There had even been a moment when she wouldn't have cared if he'd pushed her down on to the floor and . . .

She shivered, violently, and immediately Paul was beside her, perching on the arm of her chair and slipping his arm about her shoulders. 'Hey, it looks as if you're getting a cold!' he exclaimed solicitously, giving her a hug. 'That's probably why you've got a headache, too. There's a lot of flu about.'

Samantha looked up at him tensely, wondering if he had any idea what was going through her head at this moment. What would he say, she wondered, if she told him what she was thinking? How would he react to the knowledge that, instead of welcoming his embrace, she was wishing it were another man's arm about her shoulders? That, when she looked at his pale hand, with its fleshy fingers and liberal covering of sun-bleached hair, resting just above her breast, she was comparing it with another man's hand. A hand that was dark-skinned and virtually hairless, with fingers that were long and hard, and possessive, yet which had looked so right against the lace-trimmed material of her blouse...

She felt a sickening wave of self-contempt. God, how could she even think such a thing? She was disgusting; shameless! And completely crazy, she acknowledged harshly. For heaven's sake, a man had virtually forced her to make love with him, and she was sitting here, mooning about what had happened as if what he had done had been perfectly acceptable. Was actually comparing that—that—bastard—with her fiancé; with Paul. If it weren't so squalid, it would be laughable. There was no comparison between Matthew Putnam and Paul. And she deserved a thrashing for even entertaining such an idea.

Nevertheless, she was inordinately grateful when Paul decided to cut the evening short. She didn't look well, he said. She should get to bed; have an early night. He'd see her tomorrow.

But, although Samantha did do as he had suggested, sleep was not something she found it easy to attain. She tossed and turned for hours, alternately too hot or too cold, depending on what direction her thoughts took her. It was useless to pretend that any self-flagellation could control the workings of her mind. She might not want to think about Matthew Putnam, but she didn't seem capable of stopping herself. And when she eventually achieved her objective her unconscious mind was prey to every treacherous emotion she possessed.

The next few days passed without incident. Samantha, who had half expected Matthew to appear at the café again, didn't know whether she was relieved or disappointed. She knew how she ought to feel, but when did life ever imitate ideology? Instead, she lived in a kind of limbo, mid-way between anticipation and apprehension. At the end of each day she was glad that she hadn't had to face her own ambivalence, but that didn't stop her from waking every morning to the same state of awareness. She would be better once that final dinner party was behind her, she decided. With that hanging over her head, how could she get on with the rest of her life?

But, when the night of the dinner party came, the affair passed off without a hitch. It was at the home of a friend of Jennifer Spellman's, and the eight members of the party were very complimentary of Samantha's efforts. So much so that she half wished she had not made such a hasty decision about refusing any future commissions. She could have accepted at least half a dozen more that evening, and she knew they were curious to know why she had decided to give it up.

Driving home later, she had to admit she had been rather foolish. But, deep down, she had secretly expected Matthew to turn up at this dinner party as well, and she had wanted the dubious satisfaction of telling him her decision. It would have been a small satisfaction, it was true, but she hoped it would have shown him what she thought of him and his friends.

It was only now that she realised how unrealistic that had been. She had placed far too much importance on what had been for him just a game. She had accused him of as much, and he hadn't denied it. So how could she have imagined he might want to pursue the connection, particularly after that embarrassing scene in his office? If it was his office. And what did it matter anyway?

She had no answers to give herself. Her mind was in turmoil, and there seemed no escape from the duplicity of her thoughts. Matthew had no intention of seeking her out again. And she should be grateful. Without the tenuous connection her catering had provided, there wasn't the faintest likelihood that their paths might cross.

Which was why she got such a shock when she came out of the café the following Monday evening and found him waiting for her. At long last the weather had changed, and the sun was still quite warm on her shoulders as she secured the front door. It made her wish she hadn't bothered to pull on the chunky thigh-length sweater over her working clothes. But she was meeting Paul after she'd been to the wholesaler's, and she expected it would be cooler later.

She hardly noticed the man leaning against the wall between the café and the newsagent's next door. People were often hanging about when she left the café. There was a bus-stop further along the High Street, and with the car park opposite it was a popular meeting place. It was only when he straightened and came towards her that she permitted him a passing glance. Then her lips parted helplessly as the breath left her lungs.

'Hello,' he said, one hand pushed deep into the pocket of a navy blue cord jacket, and the other gripping the portfolio she had dropped in his office a week ago.

Samantha struggled to find her voice. It surfaced at last, but her answering, 'Hello,' held none of the aggression she had been nurturing towards him. She tried again, this time with more success. 'What do you want?'

Matthew shrugged. 'I came to see you, obviously.' He lifted the portfolio. 'And to return this, of course.'

'You took your time.' Samantha was ungracious, but she couldn't help it. She held out her hand. 'Thanks.'

'My pleasure.' He glanced round. 'Are you on your own?'

Samantha held up her head. 'Why shouldn't I be?'

'The girl—what was it she said she called herself——?'

'Do you mean Debbie?'

'Yes. That's right. Debbie. Isn't she with you?'

'Obviously not.' Samantha stiffened. 'She goes early to catch her bus.' She hesitated. 'Why? What do you want with Debbie?'

A lazy smile deepened the lines that fanned out from his eyes. 'Jealous?' he queried, with stomach-wrenching accuracy, and Samantha swung abruptly away. He was not going to make a fool of her a second time, she thought, despising herself for even giving him the chance. Whatever he was doing here, she wanted no part of it.

'Hey, Sam——'

But his protest went unheeded as she stood at the kerb, waiting for a gap in the traffic so that she could cross. She couldn't wait to put the width of the street between them, and it was just her luck that the traffic lights had changed against her.

'Sam,' he said, coming after her, and taking hold of her arm. 'We have to talk.'

'No, we don't.' She tried to shake him off without success, and her jaw jutted frustratedly. 'You know, it did cross my mind that you might have come to apologise, but you didn't, did you?'

'Apologise?' Clearly, the idea had never even occurred to him. 'Well—OK. If that's what you want.' He grimaced. 'I apologise.'

Samantha seethed. 'You don't mean that!' she exclaimed. 'You're only saying it to pacify me!'

'Whatever it takes,' he agreed infuriatingly. And then his eyes dropped to her mouth. 'Don't go.'

Samamtha's breathing felt suddenly constricted. 'I—I have to,' she stammered, but he only applied a little more pressure to her arm, and drew her back until her shoulder nudged his chest. His jacket was unbuttoned, and the heat of his body was palpable through the thin cotton shirt he was wearing.

'No, you don't,' he said, his warm breath lifting the hairs on her forehead. 'Come on, Sam. I've thought about little else but you for the past six days. Don't tell me you haven't thought about me—just a little, hmm?'

Samantha caught her breath. 'Will you let me go?'

'Will you not run away if I do?'

She caught her lower lip between her teeth, then she nodded her head, and to her relief he released her. It enabled her to widen the gap between them, and she inhaled several times before saying, 'You shouldn't have come here. You're wasting your time!'

'I know.' His lips twitched. 'You don't do ethnic food!'

Samantha gasped. 'Can't you ever be serious?'

His eyes darkened. 'I'd like to be.'

'Oh, God!' She dragged her eyes away from his, and looked about her. That wasn't what she had meant, and he knew it. 'Mr Putnam——'

'Matt.'

'Mr Putnam!' She shook her head. 'What do you want from me?'

'Let's go somewhere, and I'll tell you.'

'No!' She was scandalised. 'This—this has got to stop.'

'Has it?'

'Yes.' She took a steadying breath, and looked at him again. 'I don't want to talk to you.'

'I don't believe that.'

Samantha made a helpless sound. This was going on too long. Cars were passing them all the time, and any one of them could be Paul's, or someone else's who knew her. And who was she going to say was talking to her?

'Don't you have any moral feelings at all?' she demanded, and he made an indifferent movement of his shoulders.

'About what?'

'About the fact that I'm engaged to be married!' she retorted hotly. 'Oh, I realise things are done differently in your world, but in mine, if a girl is engaged to be married to one man, she doesn't play around with another!'

His brows descended. 'And what makes you think things are done differently where I come from?'

'Because they are.' Samantha hesitated. 'I—I saw you.'

'Saw me?' He looked confused. 'Saw me—what?'

'With—with that woman. Miss Mainwaring. I saw you together.'

'Yes?' He still didn't appear to understand. 'And what did you see?'

Samantha felt the colour invade her cheeks. 'That doesn't matter.'

'I think it does.'

'Oh, for heaven's sake!' Samantha's hands clenched round the portfolio. 'I have no intention of satisfying some perversive streak in your nature. Let's just say, you weren't exactly strangers to one another.'

'No, we weren't. We aren't.' Matthew expelled his breath rather heavily. 'At one time, Melissa thought she was going to marry me. Does that make it easier for you?'

'Oh!' Samantha knew a sudden weakness in the pit of her stomach. 'I—see.'

'Do you? I doubt it.' His tone was ironic now, as he closed the space between them, and looked down at her. 'Look—I need a drink. Come with me.'

Samantha bit her lip. 'I don't drink and drive.'

'A lemonade, then.'

That was said with rather less tolerance. He was losing patience. She could see it in the faint lines of tension that bracketed his mouth. She had only to wait long enough and he would get tired of humouring her. He would realise she meant what she said. She wasn't like Melissa Mainwaring. She had principles. But—oh, God!—how smug she sounded.

'Sam, please!'

The rough appeal in his voice raked her already crumbling defences. She wanted to tell him to go; to do the right thing; to prove to herself, if no one else, that everything was still the same as before. Only it wasn't. It couldn't be. No matter how she tried to deny it, things had changed. *She* had changed.

The truth was, unprincipled or not, she wanted to accept his invitation. And she knew that if she refused he would never ask her again. This was her last chance. And what was one drink, after all? It wasn't as if it meant anything. As he had said the last time he came to the café, he wasn't asking her to go to bed with him!

'I—all right,' she said, regretting the words as soon as they were uttered. It suddenly seemed quite unpardonable to accept a drink from a man who had proved to be so dishonest. Had she forgotten the way he had tricked her into going to his office? And what about his behaviour while she was there?

'OK.' His response to her acceptance was obviously relieved. She guessed he wasn't used to rejection, in any form. 'The car's parked just round the corner. In—Pilgrim Street, is that right?'

'The car?' Samantha blinked. 'I thought you just invited me for a drink.'

'I did.'

'Well?'

He pushed his hands back into his pockets. 'You think we should go into one of these pubs in the High Street?' He grimaced. 'If that's what you want.'

It wasn't. Samantha pressed her lips together. The pubs around the Market Square did not have a particularly salubrious reputation. It would be just her luck to be seen coming out of one of them with Matthew Putnam. Damned on two counts, instead of just one.

'I suppose you know somewhere better,' she challenged, deciding to let him think he would have to persuade her, but he merely fell into step beside her, and shook his head.

'It's immaterial to me,' he replied, and she gazed at him frustratedly. 'You choose,' he added. 'You know better than me.'

Samantha suppressed a groan. She should have known. A man like Matthew Putnam was unlikely to fall for her little schemes. He was far too experienced for that.

'We'll go somewhere else,' she muttered in an undertone, and he glanced sideways at her.

'Come again.'

She knew he had heard her the first time, but she had to repeat herself, and Matthew's mouth twisted in a most infuriating way.

Pilgrim Street was log-jammed, not least because of the black Porsche that was parked half on the pavement and half on double yellow lines. It was causing the traffic turning out of Pilgrim Street into the High Street to cross into the incoming lane, and at rush hour the holdup was totally unforgivable.

'Who would park——?' Samantha was beginning disgustedly, when Matthew left her to walk round the car and unlock it. 'I should have known,' she muttered grimly, as the driver trapped behind the Porsche raised his hand in an explicit signal. Then, when Matthew pushed open the passenger door from inside, she hurriedly took her seat. She just hoped no one had recognised her. It was going to be hard enough to explain.

The Porsche moved off at the first break in the traffic, and Samantha, who was still smarting from the insulting gesture she had had to suffer, gave a resentful snort. What was she doing here? she asked herself disbelievingly. Risking everything she cared about for a crazy impulse.

'It's a cliché, I know,' remarked Matthew, evidently misunderstanding her reaction, 'but it's not mine. It's Rob's. My—a friend's. He likes obvious status symbols. I don't.'

Samantha noticed her skirt had ridden up almost to her thighs, in the hasty scramble into the car, and endeavoured to inch it down. 'Don't tell me—you drive a Robin Reliant,' she retorted, in no mood to be friendly.

And then felt a curl of raw awareness in her stomach when he gave a husky laugh.

'Not exactly,' he replied, glancing sideways at her, and she knew he had observed her awkward manoeuvrings. 'Driving in London is pretty hopeless, anyway. As no doubt you know in your business.'

'It's not my business,' said Samantha shortly, giving up any attempt to be circumspect, and tugging forcefully at her hemline. 'Not any more. I've given up working for other people.'

'Why?'

Matthew was negotiating the roadworks in Falls Way as he spoke, but that didn't stop him from giving her a curious look. It was her opportunity to tell him exactly what part he'd played in her decision, but for some reason she chose not to. Why should she give him the satisfaction of knowing he was responsible? she argued. It really was nothing to do with him. It was her fault for being so naïve.

'Because—because the only time I see my fiancé is in the evenings, and it was taking up too much time,' she said at last. 'Um—where are we going? I can't be too long, you know.'

Matthew's mouth turned down. 'Because you're meeting your fiancé, I suppose.'

'As a matter of fact, yes.'

He nodded. 'Will this do, then?' he asked, indicating the swinging sign of a pub on the outskirts of the town, his tone considerably cooler. 'The Black Raven! That sounds appropriate.'

Samantha didn't answer him, and Matthew swung the sleek sports car into the car park and brought it to a restrained halt. 'OK,' he said, thrusting open his door and swinging his long legs out of the vehicle. 'Let's hope they serve their Scotch in generous measures.'

Samantha struggled out with as little dignity as she'd got in. But she didn't want him coming round to help her. 'You shouldn't drink——'

'—and drive, I know,' he finished for her tersely. 'Don't worry, *mou kardhia*. My constitution is quite used to it.'

Samantha frowned as he locked the door. 'Moo—moo, what?' she echoed, having heard nothing after that rather musical address.

'*Mou kardhia*,' he repeated, making the second half of the first word sound like *e*. 'It's Greek,' he added flatly. He nodded towards the entrance. 'Shall we go in?'

Samantha blinked, but when he started towards the open door she hurried after him. 'Greek,' she said, a little breathlessly. 'Do you speak Greek?' She shook her head. 'How—clever of you.'

'Not really. My mother's Greek,' he informed her carelessly. And then, pausing in the narrow hallway of the hotel, 'Bar or lounge? It's up to you.'

Samantha left the decision to him, and then wished she hadn't when they ended up in a dark booth in a corner of the smoky bar. Exactly the sort of place she had imagined he would choose, she thought irritably, as he took the seat opposite. The only difference was that his knees brushed hers, instead of his thigh, but she quickly moved her legs to avoid that situation.

She had asked for a mineral water, and, although Matthew had given her a wry look when she did so, that was what he set in front of her. For himself, he had a foaming glass of the local brew, and Samantha couldn't help her look of surprise when he set the glass on the table.

'So I took your advice,' he remarked, after she had shifted out of his way. 'Is this what your fiancé drinks? Real ale?'

Samantha didn't particularly want to be reminded about Paul at this moment, and her shoulders stiffened. 'Yes, as a matter of fact,' she retorted, resenting the disparaging way he said it. 'But I'm sure you're not interested in what Paul drinks.'

'On the contrary.' He took a mouthful of the beer and wiped the back of his hand across his mouth. 'I'm interested in everything about you. Including your fiancé.'

'Have you no shame?'

The words burst from her, and he expelled a resigned breath. 'Apparently not. Where you're concerned,' he appended ruefully. 'Does that damn me in your eyes?'

Samantha chose not to answer that and, after a moment, he said gently, 'Tell me about you; about what you like to do. Whose idea was it to open the café?' He paused. 'Paul's?'

'Yes, as a matter of fact.' Samantha pressed her lips together. 'Paul—supports me a lot. In—in everything.'

'Except when it interferes with his time with you.'

'What do you mean?'

'He forced you to give up the outside catering, didn't he?' Matthew reminded her mildly, and she guessed he had used those words deliberately. 'Which is a pity, because I—had a commission for you.'

She was tempted to tell him that he had had more to do with her giving up the catering than Paul had, but that would have been playing into his hands once again. So, instead, she said, 'Another one?' managing to sound almost as disparaging as he had sounded earlier.

'Hmm.'

Matthew looked into his drink, stroking one long finger down the condensation on his glass. In spite of herself, it reminded her of those same fingers sliding down the quivering column of her throat. She experienced almost the same sensation, and when he lifted his heavy lids and intercepted her gaze she suspected he was thinking of it, too.

'What's he like?' he asked huskily, and for a moment she was too mesmerised to speak.

'I—I beg—your——'

'Paul,' he prompted, cradling the glass between his palms. 'Does he make you happy? In bed, I mean,' he added incredibly. 'Because I have to tell you, I don't think he does.'

'You know nothing about——'

'If I didn't know better, I'd say you were totally inexperienced,' he went on, as if she hadn't said anything. 'He must be a rank amateur, that's all I can say.'

'I don't think you'd better say anything else,' hissed Samantha, clutching her glass. 'Not unless you want me to throw this over you.'

Matthew shrugged. 'So what are you doing here with me?'

Samantha gasped. That he should ask her *that*! When he had practically *kidnapped* her outside the café! Forget the fact that she had agreed to come with him of her own accord. It was his fault she was here, and that was that.

'I think you'd better take me back to town,' she declared unsteadily, but when she would have slid out of the booth his thigh was in the way.

'Don't do this,' he implored wearily. 'Not again.' He captured her trembling hands. 'All right. That was unforgivable. I apologise. Now, will you cool down?'

'No.' Her eyes sparkled resentfully. 'I should have known better than to expect any kind of respect from you! You just enjoy tormenting me, don't you?'

His eyes darkened. 'There are things we'd both enjoy a hell of a lot more,' he told her shortly. And then, before she could comprehend what he was doing, he had levered his lean frame out of his side of the booth and into hers. His arm went along the back of her seat, and it took all her will-power to resist the urge to try and melt into the woodwork. 'Let's both stop playing games, shall we?' he murmured, his free hand turning her face to his. His thumb brushed sensually across her parted lips. 'Do you have any idea what I want to do at this moment?'

Samantha breathed unevenly. There didn't seem to be enough air in the booth, and every time she tried to fill her lungs she was intensely conscious of her full breasts straining at the lacy confines of her bra. She rather thought he was aware of it, too, and there was a frankly sensual curve to his mouth as he watched her agitation.

'Do you?' he prompted again, and she moved her head in a helpless sideways gesture.

'I've got to go,' she said instead, glancing half apprehensively towards the bar, but the bartender was busy, and no one was paying any attention to them.

'No, you don't,' he contradicted her gently, bending his head and touching the sensitive hollow beneath her ear with his tongue. 'Be honest: you want to stay.' He took the lobe of her ear between his teeth and bit it. 'You just feel guilty, that's all.'

'Yes, I do.' She latched on to that statement like a drowning woman. 'I shouldn't be here. I shouldn't have come here. I want you to take me back.'

Matthew sighed, his hand falling away on to her lap. It was where her two hands were clasped together, but she didn't allow him to take hold of them again. Instead, she gripped the banquette on either side of her, cooling her hot palms, and digging her nails into the coarse cloth.

She was aware of him watching her; she was aware of the strong hand lying weightily against her knees. She was also aware that she was exuding moisture from every pore of her body, and that between her legs a pulse was beating wildly.

'I'll take you back,' he said at last, and she wondered why that news didn't give her the relief it should. 'But I think you should listen to what I have to say first,' he added, turning his hand over and testing its strength against her taut thigh. 'It's my grandfather's birthday at the end of this month. On Easter Saturday, actually. My mother is giving a party for him, and I suggested that you might be willing to help her.'

Samantha's breath caught in her throat. 'Your—your grandfather?' she got out, in a high, unnatural voice, and Matthew inclined his head.

'Hmm,' he said, flexing his fingers against her leg. He looked down as his knuckles brushed the hem of her short black skirt, but instead of withdrawing his hand he slid it back and forth against the ribbed mesh of her black tights. 'I guess we're talking about fifty people, or thereabouts.' His eyes sought hers. 'A family get-together. What do you think?'

Samantha swallowed, a convulsive movement of her throat that owed more to the sensitised state of her body than to any sense of consternation at the numbers. 'I— couldn't cater for fifty people,' she protested weakly, but his lazy smile sent a shaft of pure, unadulterated hunger through her shaking body.

'No one's asking you to,' he murmured, taking advantage of her parted lips and tracing their softness with his tongue. 'She just needs someone to help her, that's all,' he went on, bestowing a light kiss at the corner of her mouth. 'I told her you'd be the ideal person.'

Samantha shivered. 'You—you said—your mother was Greek,' she stammered, torn between the desire to destroy this intimacy once and for all, and the aching wish that he would kiss her properly, and put her out of her misery. 'Wh-where do she and—and your grandfather—live?'

'In Greece, of course,' he declared, shattering her hopes and reaching for his drink. 'Well? Will you do it?'

CHAPTER SIX

MATTHEW came up out of the ocean, shaking water from every limb. At this hour of the morning the sea was icy cold and refreshing, still harbouring the cool temperatures of winter, and not yet tempered by the already strengthening sun.

He swept his hair back with a careless hand, and squeezed moisture from where it clung to the back of his neck. The cold drops ran down over his muscled shoulders and disappeared into the waistband of the shorts he had worn to sleep in, and he shivered. But it felt good to be alive, and a lazy hand confirmed that the thickening at his midriff had been checked. Since he had cut down on his drinking and started exercising again, his health had improved considerably, and he could face each morning without the recurring hangover he had grown to accept.

And he owed at least part of it to Samantha, he reflected ruefully, feeling his body stir as it always did when he thought of her. But, in the thin shorts, his reaction was unwelcome, particularly as he could see his grandfather sitting on the terrace waiting for him. The old man always rose at six. He had forgotten about that. It was his mother he had been thinking of when he'd kept his shorts on for swimming. But his grandfather had arrived the night before, and now Matthew was glad he had decided to show some respect.

He had left a towel lying on the sand, and now he picked it up and took a moment to dry his head and shoulders. Then, knotting it loosely about his waist, he crossed the fine sand to the steps that led up to the terrace.

'Papa,' he addressed the old man politely, and Aristotle Apollonius inclined his grey head in a look that mingled slight displeasure with reluctant pride.

'Matthew,' he accorded, gesturing to the cushioned chair at the other side of the lacquered wrought-iron table. 'You did not use to be such an early riser.'

'No,' Matthew acknowledged the faint censure in his grandfather's tone, and although he would have preferred to go straight into the villa for his shower he humoured him and sat down. 'The water's very inviting.'

His grandfather had spoken in Greek, and, although Matthew knew the old man could speak English as well as he could, he responded in the same language. He had no wish to get into an argument over his rejection of his mother's culture in favour of his father's. Not when there was already a rift between them big enough to double the Marianas Trench.

'Are you sure it is not the imminent arrival of this young woman—what did you say her name was? Max-Maxell?'

'Maxwell,' corrected Matthew patiently, knowing that a man who could recite the tonnage of a hundred oil tankers at a stroke was unlikely to be daunted by one surname. 'Her name's Samantha Maxwell. I believe my mother told you that several days ago.'

'She may have done.' Aristotle was dismissive. 'But I cannot be expected to remember the name of every female you sleep with.'

Matthew's mouth compressed. 'Did my mother tell you I was sleeping with her?' he enquired pleasantly, and his grandfather shifted somewhat uncomfortably.

'I do not know,' he responded, adjusting the collar of his white linen jacket. 'She may have done. As I say, I do not always remember.'

Matthew gave him an old-fashioned look. 'Really? I doubt if you'd like your competitors to hear that,' he remarked, leaning forward, legs apart, his forearms along his thighs. 'Are you getting old, Papa?'

'Yes, I am.' The old man's eyes flashed with sudden anger. 'And what do you care? My one and only grandson? I have to have a birthday before you can find the time to see me!'

'That's not true.' Matthew breathed out on a sigh. 'I came to see you—three months ago. In Athens.'

'Did you? Did you?' Aristotle's lips twisted. 'As I recall it, you were drunk at least three-quarters of the time you were there. And you slept the rest!'

'Yes, well——' Matthew felt a momentary sense of guilt. 'That was different.'

'How was it different?' The old man sneered. 'You were drunk because some little tart refused to spread her legs for you! Your mother told me. She had sympathy for you. I did not.'

Matthew's jaw tightened. 'Did I ask for your sympathy?' he demanded, as, just for a moment, the familiar sense of bereavement he had felt at Melissa's betrayal gripped him.

'No.' His grandfather expelled the word with raw frustration. 'But that doesn't mean I forgive you. Or that I'll feel any different this time, when the Maxwell girl realises she's wasting her time.'

Matthew suppressed a sudden urge to lash out at the old man and lay back in his chair, determinedly crossing one ankle across his knee. 'That won't happen,' he declared flatly, watching as sunspots appeared on the blue, blue waters of the small bay. 'And, just for your information, I haven't slept with her. Yet.'

'But you intend to.'

Matthew's mouth twisted. 'Yes. I intend to.'

His grandfather grimaced, taking a Cellophane-covered cigar out of his breast pocket, and peeling the wrapper. He trimmed it with a gold clipper and felt about in his pockets for some matches. 'Who is she anyway?' he snapped, discovering a book of matches, with the logo of an exclusive Athens nightclub on the flap, and striking one irritably. 'Caroline says she's a waitress.' He puffed at the cigar. 'Cannot you find enough women of your own class, without getting involved with a *waitress*?'

'I didn't realise you were a snob, Papa,' Matthew countered evenly, though he was finding it increasingly difficult to keep his temper. 'And, as it happens, she's not a waitress. As my mother knows, and as I'm sure she's told you, Sam runs a small café. And—until recently—she did some outside catering, too. I'd have thought you'd admire initiative. You've always told me that that was how you made your fortune. And speaking of class——'

'That will do, Matthew.' His mother's voice overrode what he had been about to say, and, although he was tempted to ignore her, his grandfather's heaving chest deterred him. 'Apollo, you know what the doctor said about smoking,' Caroline added, whisking the cigar out of her father's hand and grinding it beneath the heel of her painted sandals. 'Now, why can't I leave you two alone for more than five minutes without finding you at each other's throats?'

'Hardly that,' remarked Matthew quietly, getting to his feet, and loosening the knot of the slipping towel. He slotted it about his shoulders. 'I need a shower. If you'll both excuse me, I'll go and wash the salt from this debauched body of mine.'

'Oh, Matthew!' His mother caught his bare arm as he passed. 'You're not—you're not planning on doing anything silly, are you, darling?'

'Silly?' Matthew looked puzzled. 'Like what?'

'Like—leaving, for example.'

'With his new mistress arriving later this morning, I should hardly think so,' put in her father drily. He pulled out another cigar. 'Let the boy go, Caroline. He and I understand one another. Which is more than you and I ever did.'

Matthew left his mother protesting that her father was going the right way to kill himself by ignoring his doctor's orders, and crossed the marble tiles into the wide entrance hall of the villa. Vine-hung, trellised walls gave this area of the house a natural airiness, and, although at the height of summer an efficient air-conditioning system came into operation, much of the building's coolness was owed to Minoan design. That ancient civilisation had believed in a through-flow of air in their homes, and many of the buildings on Delphus still imitated these fundamental principles.

Not that the rest of his grandfather's villa could be said to resemble any ancient precepts, Matthew mused as he walked along an arched corridor to his own suite of rooms. Beneath his bare feet, the mosaic of Italian marble was strewn with soft Bokhara rugs, and the walls beside him had been decorated by a master hand. Expertly etched murals, in jewel-bright colours, reflected the du-ality of his grandfather's history. His father, Matthew's great-grandfather, had had his origins in the deserts of North Africa, and although the old man didn't like to be reminded of his Arab antecedents he couldn't deny his love of Moorish architecture.

And there was plenty of room here for him to indulge in whatever style of architecture took his fancy, thought Matthew, pushing open the heavy-panelled door into his sitting-room. Built in the days when his grandfather had hoped to have a large family, it sprawled over more than an acre, with halls and reception-rooms of mammoth proportions. The twenty or so guest suites had all been designed to take advantage of the villa's surroundings, and, stepping out into flower-filled courtyards, you were immediately assailed by the absolute perfection of the view. From its position on a rocky promontory the villa was surrounded on three sides by the sparkling waters of the Aegean, and, for all his ambivalence about coming here, Matthew accepted there was nowhere more uniquely placed.

That he didn't come as often as he should was a source of both bitterness and frustration to his grandfather. But then, Matthew conceded with a trace of self-mockery, he had always been something of a disappointment to the old man. Who else, born into a shipping dynasty, would have chosen to ignore all the benefits his grandfather's wealth could give him, and start his own company? Who else would have gone against the strength of his grand-father's will, and clung to the admittedly weaker link of his father's heritage?

The trouble was, he had never been able to explain his reasons to the old man. Aristotle—*Apollo*—whatever he cared to call himself, had never had the time to listen to

his grandson's opinions. Well, not when he had needed
to voice them, anyway, Matthew amended now, stepping out of his wet shorts, and padding into the
Byzantine luxury of the bathroom.

Growing up in his grandfather's house in Athens, a
house necessarily protected from the outside world, he
had longed to escape; to be like the children who played
beyond the electrified gates that kept him a prisoner.
Going to school in England had been a revelation, for, no
matter how his grandfather might resent the system his
father had chosen for him, the boarding school in
Hertfordshire had been far from the old man's influence. That was when Matthew had started to rebel. That
was when he had started to fight the stifling control of his
mother's family. He didn't want the responsibilities his
grandfather would have put on him. He didn't want to
live in a world where bodyguards were an accepted part
of life and every move he made was reported on. He
wanted freedom, and choices. He wanted to be Matthew
Putnam; not Matthew Apollonius.

Of course, it hadn't been easy. There had been threats
from his grandfather, and tears from his mother. But he
had done it. He had made a life for himself, forged his
own destiny—if only temporarily, he allowed with a certain irony. He knew that, sooner or later, fate would
catch up with him. He was his grandfather's heir. Victor's
presence was a constant reminder. And, while he might
succeed in eluding his responsibilities for a while longer,
much of his future was tied up in bills of lading at
Piraeus.

He sighed, tilting his face up to the hot spray of water
that cascaded from a decidedly modern faucet. Its pum-
melling force put feeling back into his shoulders, which
had become chilled during his conversation with his

grandfather. *Conversation?* He pulled a wry face. Confrontation, more like.

But, for all that, bringing Samantha here was undoubtedly an unwise move. Not only as far as his grandfather's blood-pressure was concerned, but also because of his own reasons for doing so. Frankly, he wasn't too sure why he had done it. It had certainly not been his intention when he'd intercepted her outside the café. But circumstances had contrived to force his hand, and although he despised the impulse that had caused him to make such a suggestion it was done now, and he had to live with it.

Nevertheless, that didn't stop him from feeling a heel. He had invited her here under false pretences; and, even if some despicable core of his anatomy welcomed the knowledge, he couldn't excuse his own behaviour.

After all, he knew his mother would never allow an outsider to interfere with her plans for the birthday celebrations. Besides, the arrangements had been completed weeks ago, with every detail honed to perfection. Apart from anything else, there was an army of servants at the villa, capable of feeding the five thousand, let alone a paltry fifty guests. It was only Samantha's lack of experience that had allowed him to pull such a stunt. But then, she still had no idea who he really was.

His lips tightened. If he had a shred of decency in him, he would tell her the truth right away, instead of letting her go on believing she had some purpose here beyond the plans he had for her. He should send her back where she had come from, no better or worse than when she left. Back to her fiancé, and her steady, boring existence.

But he knew he wouldn't do it. She was sensitive, and naïve—and incredibly innocent—and he was about to ruin her life. He was using her to expunge his frustration over Melissa, but for the first time in weeks he felt alive again. She had done that for him. And it wasn't as if she was indifferent to him. God, he had known that night in the pub that she was vulnerable. All that defensive indignation! It had all been an act. If she hadn't wanted to see him again, he wouldn't have forced her. But it had taken so little persuasion to change her mind...

With an impatient hand he switched the temperature control to cold. He felt hot now, hot and ridiculously excited, considering it was more than fifteen years since a contemporary of his mother's had taught him how to please a woman. And, incidentally, how to please himself, too, he recalled, turning off the tap, and tugging a thick bathsheet from the rack. It was years since he had remembered that initiation, but since then several women had benefited from the experience. And Samantha...

He frowned. What time was it? he wondered. He had taken his watch off before he went for his swim, and now he wrapped the towel about him and went into his bedroom.

It was lying amid the tumbled sheets of the enormous bed, which occupied a bare quarter of the floor-space in the huge, high-ceilinged apartment. A tapestry quilt in shades of green and gold was lying in a heap on the floor, and he heaved it back on to the bed before picking up the timepiece. It was still early, he saw. Barely seven o'clock. Samantha wouldn't be arriving for another five hours, at least. Always supposing she didn't get cold feet at the last minute and let the plane go without her, he brooded tersely. But no. She wouldn't do that. She had said she would come, and she would. She trusted him.

*   *   *

Samantha didn't know what she had expected to happen when she landed in Greece, but being met by a complete stranger had definitely not figured in her plans.

When Matthew had sent her a return ticket to Athens, with the flight number and time of departure clearly indicated, she had naturally assumed he intended to meet her at the airport himself. Beyond telling her that Delphus, the place where his mother and grandfather lived, was some distance from Athens, he had given no details of how she was supposed to get there. Which was why she had expected he was going to meet her. Surely he must know how nervous she was.

But instead she had been met by an admittedly trust worthy-looking individual in a pilot's uniform, who introduced himself as Spiro Niarchos. He had explained, somewhat confusingly, that he worked for the Apollonius Corporation, and that he had been sent to escort her to her destination.

Samantha had had little choice but to go with him. Even if, at that time, her interpretation of his uniform had run along the lines of its being that of a chauffeur. But, instead of a limousine, he had escorted her to a gleaming blue and silver helicopter, with the logo of the Apollonius Corporation emblazoned on its side.

Now, some distance out over the blue-green waters of what she had guessed was the Aegean, her earlier doubts and fears had congealed into a tight knot of apprehension inside her. Where were they really going? she wondered. And would his mother and his grandfather really be there when they arrived? And if they weren't, what was she going to do about it? She had agreed to come, knowing full well that Matthew Putnam wanted more than her professional services.

Dear God!

She closed her eyes for a moment as the enormity of what she had done washed over her. It was no use telling herself that so far as Paul and her parents were concerned this was just another assignment, when she knew it wasn't. Just because she had managed to persuade them that this was an opportunity she couldn't turn down didn't alter the fact of her duplicity. She had told lies; invented excuses; even used her friendship with Jennifer Spellman to justify what she was doing. And why? Because she was *mad*, that was why. Mad to even think that a man like Matthew Putnam really cared anything about her. And yet . . .

She opened her eyes again on a scene of breathtaking loveliness. It wasn't like flying in an aeroplane, which reduced everything to matchbox proportions. From the windows of the helicopter she could see even the smallest island, and yachts and other sailing craft, cruising these land-locked waters.

So, she acknowledged tensely, Matthew's family must live on one of these islands. Remembering what she knew of Greek geography, she guessed his grandfather must be either a fisherman or a farmer. Probably the former, she decided thoughtfully, running her tongue over her lower lip. Unless the island was bigger than she expected—and, as she'd never heard of it, that didn't seem likely—there didn't seem a lot of room for cultivation. The smaller islands they were passing over were rocky outcrops in the main, with just a few sheep, and a handful of fig or olive trees providing shade. Not the kind of place to hold a party for fifty people, she would have thought. But then, she didn't really know what kind of party it was going to be.

She sighed uneasily. The conviction that she was making a terrible mistake by coming here was growing stronger by the minute. What did she know of Greek people? What did she know of Greek food? She had read somewhere that the Greeks were very hospitable. But the article had been concerned with tourism, not with a single Englishwoman venturing into the unknown.

She glanced sideways at the pilot and noticed that his uniform bore the Apollonius Corporation logo, too. What did it all mean? The name was vaguely familiar to her, and she thought she remembered hearing it used in connection with shipping. But why would a helicopter belonging to a shipping company be transporting her to Delphus? Unless, Matthew's company, J.P. Software, was part of the Apollonius Corporation, too.

The more she thought about it, the more logical it sounded. It explained so much, not least the helicopter, and Matthew's apparent thoughtlessness at not meeting her in Athens. And she should be feeling grateful that she was not having to spend several hours on an inter-island ferry. Judging by the distance they had flown, it would have probably taken the rest of the day by sea. Even so...

She pressed surreptitious hands against her churning stomach. The fact remained, she was still taking an enormous risk by coming here. She knew nothing of Matthew's family, and hardly more about himself. Could she really pretend his motives were honourable, when he'd virtually admitted they weren't? And what did she want anyway? Her future was in Northfleet, with Paul.

Desperate to escape the downward spiral on which her thoughts were taking her, Samantha turned to look at the pilot again. She was sitting beside him, in the front of the aircraft, and because the engines were noisy she had to speak to him by means of the microphone that was attached to the helmet he had given her to wear.

'Are we nearly there?' she asked, hoping his English didn't just stretch to the formal greeting and necessary instructions he had issued earlier.

'Almost,' he conceded, polite but unforthcoming, and although she sensed his reticence she persevered.

'Does—er—does Mr Putnam often use the helicopter?'

It was a stupid question, and she hoped he didn't think she was trying to find out if he had brought any other young women to the island. Besides which, Matthew wasn't exactly using the helicopter, was he? She didn't honestly know if he ever had.

The pilot's expression as he looked at her mirrored her own uncertainty, and she was convinced he was wondering what Matthew saw in her. But then, almost indifferently, it seemed, he shrugged his shoulders, and returned his attention to flying the aircraft.

'It is—at his disposal, whenever he wishes it,' he said, after a lengthy hesitation, and Samantha, who had decided he was not going to answer her, caught her breath. 'But, as he lives in England,' Spiro Niarchos continued slowly, 'I am employed most frequently by his mother.'

Samantha gulped. '*His mother*!'

'*Ne*. Kyria Putnam.' He paused, and then added, politely, 'You have met *Mrs* Putnam, have you not?'

'No. No, I haven't.'

Samantha answered almost absently, her mind racing with the possibilities his casual words had created. Who was Matthew's mother, if she used a helicopter to get around in? And why hadn't he warned her that this was no ordinary family?

It was her own fault, she thought miserably. She should have insisted on some answers before agreeing to this trip. But, although she had suspected that anyone who gave a party for fifty people had to be fairly well off, she had never imagined anything like this.

The truth was, she had been so wrapped up with her own guilt at deceiving Paul that everything else had assumed a lesser importance. The only people who had figured strongly in her thoughts were herself and Matthew, and it wasn't until Spiro Niarchos had spoken of Matthew's mother that she had realised how naïve she had been.

What was she doing here? she asked herself again. What gave her the right to play fast and loose with her relationship with Paul, which had lasted more than six years? If she had wanted a taste of excitement—and she could think of no other excuse for what she was doing— she should have chosen someone in her own league. Not allowed herself to get entangled with a man whose background became more intimidating by the minute.

'We will be landing in less than fifteen minutes,' Spiro told her a little while later, and Samantha curled her nails into her damp palms. What would he do, she wondered, if she asked him to turn round, and fly her back to Athens? Probably refuse, she decided glumly. And it didn't matter anyway. She didn't have the nerve to suggest it.

They were flying diagonally into the sun now, and the light on the water was dazzling. Below the helicopter she could see the swell that ran before the bow of a gleaming schooner, and as they swept in lower she saw a man on water-skis, zigzagging in the wake of a launch.

She stared, but the man wasn't Matthew, even if he did have the same dark skin. He was older, too. Probably in his late forties, or early fifties, with a stocky, well-fed physique that spoke of too many liquid lunches. A relative, perhaps, she guessed tautly, having to abandon her

theory that Matthew's grandfather might be a fisherman. She drew her lower lip between her teeth, and bit
down, hard. It served her right for telling lies, she
thought unhappily. Nothing good ever came from trying
to cheat fate.

The island was beneath them now, and in spite of her
misgivings Samantha gazed down at it intently. It wasn't
large, but it was bigger than she had expected, with lush
green slopes tapering down to the shimmering waters of
the Aegean. At the northern end of the island a cluster of
white-painted buildings hugged a narrow inlet, which was
apparently the only means of access by sea. Samantha
glimpsed several fishing boats moored in the harbour,
and the bell-tower of a church, before the helicopter
swept her south again, towards a broad, jutting peninsula.

There was a house on the peninsula; or perhaps it was
a hotel, she speculated nervously, no longer sure of anything in the present situation. It was painted white, too,
a brilliant, blistering white that made her eyes ache, with
turrets and arches, giving it the look of a medieval pal-
ace. Whatever it was, it seemed to spread in all direc-
tions, with flower-filled courtyards, tennis courts, and
vine-hung terraces, above acres of coarse brown sand.

It was evidently their destination, and her stomach
clenched in sudden panic as Spiro lowered the helicopter
on to a custom-build pad maybe a quarter of a mile from
the house. If he was aware of her strained reaction to
their arrival he was polite enough not to mention it, and
in any case Samantha was immediately diverted by the
sight of a man lounging on a stone wall, just yards from
where the aircraft landed.

It was Matthew. She recognised him instantly, and she
didn't know whether she felt angry or relieved. In all

honesty, she didn't know how she felt, and although she had to get out of the helicopter her legs felt ridiculously weak.

She suspected it was seeing him again. She hadn't laid eyes on him since the evening when he had persuaded her to come here, and although she had spoken to him once on the phone it wasn't the same. And he wasn't the same either, she fretted, as he pushed himself up from the pile of stones, and strolled, barefoot, towards the helicopter. In frayed denim shorts and nothing else, with the sun beating down on his exposed head and shoulders, he looked little like the man she remembered. Seeing him now, like this, she could quite believe he wasn't wholly English. Indeed, he looked totally alien, and only the lazy smile that tugged at the corners of his mouth betrayed his identity.

Perhaps she was wrong, she thought desperately. Perhaps, even now, she was making a mistake. It was always possible that his mother worked at the house— *hotel*—behind them. After all, he didn't look anything like the wealthy playboy she had seen water-skiing . . .

'Hi, Spiro!' Matthew had reached the helicopter now, and was jerking open the door at her side. His gaze flicked swiftly over her tense face, and then he returned his attention to the pilot. 'No problem?'

'No. No problem.'

Spiro responded with obvious warmth, and Samantha, covertly observing the exchange of looks between them, knew her worst fears were being realised. For, in spite of Spiro's cordiality, there was a definite note of respect in his voice. The kind of respect he might have for his employer, she determined anxiously. Oh, lord, why hadn't Matthew warned her?

'Good!' Matthew's gaze moved back to her stiff form. 'Sam,' he added, in a low voice. 'Do you need any help?'

Not from you!

The words trembled unspoken between them, and Samantha knew he was as conscious of her hostility as she was. That was why he hadn't wasted any time in lengthy greetings. He must know as well as she did that she didn't want to get out at all.

But she couldn't stay in the helicopter indefinitely. Spiro was apparently waiting to take off again, and she was obliged to make a move. Taking off the helmet, she placed it carefully on the console, and then, uncaring of how she looked, she swung her legs out of the aircraft.

She narrowly missed winding Matthew by her unexpected action, but his fingers grasped her elbow when she dropped the few inches to the concrete apron.

'I can manage,' she snapped as soon as she had regained her balance, and Matthew merely raised his eyebrows before turning to help Spiro with her luggage.

She had only brought one suitcase and a canvas flight bag, and Matthew hefted them easily. *'Tha idhothoume avrio,'* he nodded, after denying he needed Spiro's help, and then, switching to English, he said, 'Let's go. Unless you want to be blown away by the propellers.'

Samantha pressed her lips together, but the logic of his argument was undeniable. The landing pad was situated just a few yards from the beach. The air was still quivering with dust from the helicopter's landing, and when it took off again...

Besides which, she had no desire to stay outside in this hot sun. She was already feeling uncomfortably warm in her jacket, and the fine woollen trousers, which had seemed so suitable in England, were now clinging damply to her legs.

The propellers began to pick up speed behind her, and she hurried the few feet to where Matthew was waiting, watching the aircraft take off. She concentrated on the helicopter in an effort to distract her gaze from Matthew's muscled torso, but she was overpoweringly conscious of him standing there beside her. It was the first time she had seen him without his city clothes—practically without any clothes at all, she amended tensely—and she was sharply aware of the width of his chest, and the hair-roughened muscles of his thighs. He looked dark—and dangerous, she conceded uneasily. And unnervingly like a stranger; someone she'd never seen before...

CHAPTER SEVEN

SAMANTHA stood at the open french doors, gazing out at the ocean. The scent of mimosa hung in the still afternoon air, and the scarlet petals of geraniums tumbled from a dozen tubs strewn about the courtyard. In the centre of the courtyard, a stone nymph spilled water from an urn she was holding into the marble basin at her feet. It meant Samantha could always hear the cooling sound of running water, and she already knew the fountain was spread with lilies at its base.

Beyond the courtyard a walled garden gave on to a flagged terrace. And, beyond the terrace, steps led down to a sandy beach. From her position by the folding glass doors Samantha had a spectacular view of blue-green waters creaming along the shoreline, with the occasional glimpse of snow-white sails, nudging the horizon.

It was all quite breathtaking, and unbelievably beautiful. And certainly nothing like she had expected. Oh, she had been prepared for the light and colour of Greece, particularly after an English winter, but the unashamed luxury of Matthew's grandfather's house had left her feeling numb and confused.

She glanced round at her suitcase lying on the carved chest at the foot of the bed. Even her luggage looked lost in these surroundings. And as out of place as she was, she acknowledged with a sigh. She should never have come here. She should never have succumbed to Matthew's sensual persuasion. How could someone who lived in this place ever require her assistance? It simply wasn't credible. It had all been just a lie.

And yet, she admitted, sliding a weary hand through her hair, she had known from the beginning that helping Matthew's mother organise his grandfather's birthday party had never been the whole reason for her trip. So why was she feeling so depressed now? Just because the circumstances were vastly different from what she had expected, why did she feel so empty, as if something precious had been taken away from her?

She sighed, and, moving away from the windows, she surveyed the cream and rose splendour of her surroundings. When she had first been shown into these rooms she had been convinced someone had made a mistake. The richly furnished sitting-room, with its soft velvet sofas and carved cabinets, could not be for her. Any more than could the huge bed, in the room adjoining, with its exotically hanging draperies, or the lavishly equipped bathroom, sporting a step-in pool deep enough to swim in. These were not the apartments of someone who had come here under false pretences. And it was certainly not the kind of accommodation she had had in mind when she had agreed to come.

Which was really what was wrong, she acknowledged dully. Until she had seen this place, she had been labouring under the not unnatural illusion that, despite Matthew's involvement with Melissa Mainwaring, he was not so different from herself. It was difficult to make sense of what she had been thinking, but she knew that, deep down, she had entertained some notion that she and Matthew might——

She drew a breath. Might what? she asked herself bitterly. Might become friends? *Lovers*? Might fall in love?

The naïveté of such thoughts appalled her now. No one who lived in a place like this could conceivably care about someone like her. Whatever he had brought her here for—and she knew now that helping his mother with anything was out of the question—it was not because he had any serious intentions towards her. He found her a diversion, and quite amusing, but apart from going to bed with her there was nothing else he wanted.

It was almost feudal really, she brooded, flicking the strap of the nightgown that was hanging half-in, half-out of the case. She had been brought here to keep Matthew amused. No expense spared—so long as she didn't get ideas above her station.

If only she had had the chance to talk to Matthew before Spiro Niarchos took off for Athens. If only she had had the chance to talk to Matthew, period. But she hadn't. No sooner had the helicopter lifted off than a smiling maid servant had appeared to escort her to her room. And, although Matthew had brought her suitcases into the house, another servant, a man this time, had relieved him of that duty too.

He must have known how she was feeling, but he made no attempt to accompany her. Instead, it had been left to the maid to show her to her suite. And, although she might have expected him to join her for a late lunch, a tray of food had been waiting for her when she emerged from the bathroom.

She supposed it was possible that he had thought she might be tired. After all, it had been very early when she'd left Northfleet, and she might have wanted to have a rest. But Samantha was too strung-up to rest, too apprehensive to sleep. Beautiful as this place undoubtedly was, she couldn't relax here.

And he must know it, she fretted, as resentment took the place of consternation. That was why he was keeping out of her way. He must know she couldn't stay here, meeting his family, and joining his grandfather's guests as if she were one of them. She wasn't. She could never be. It was just another of his games, and she had been foolish enough to fall for it.

Of course, she conceded tightly, glancing down at the chainstore-bought cotton trousers and vest-top she had changed into for coolness, he might have no intention of introducing her to his family. Just because she had been given a luxurious place to stay was no guarantee that she was to be treated like all the other guests. This might be as much of the villa as she was intended to see. Her own sitting-room; her own private courtyard! Why should she assume she'd be invited to join the family?

She glanced down at her watch. It was four o'clock, she saw unhappily, taking a choked breath. If she hadn't thought someone might see her, she'd have gone for a walk on the beach. Anything to get away from this gilded cage, and the disturbing images it created.

Of course, she could always finish her unpacking, she thought bitterly, realising that, whatever happened, she wasn't going to find it easy to get away from here before the party was over. But the party wasn't until tomorrow night, and there were an awful lot of hours between.

She heard a sound from the sitting-room next door, and her mouth went dry. But when no one called her name she expelled an uneven breath. No doubt someone had come to take away the untouched tray, she thought despairingly. But she hadn't been able to eat a thing, not with God knew what hanging over her head.

'Feeling better?'

The softly spoken enquiry startled her, and Samantha
swung round almost guiltily. Not that she had anything
to be guilty of, she assured herself grimly. Not with these
people, at least. And when she saw Matthew standing in
the arched doorway to the sitting-room her most immediate feelings were those of frustration.

All the same, she was instantly receptive to his dark
sexuality, which was only enhanced by the narrow-fitting
chinos he was wearing. They accentuated the powerful
length of his legs, moulding his thighs, and stretching
taut across his sex. Samantha looked once, and then
away, forcing herself to concentrate on a point somewhere to the left of his right ear.

And, 'No,' she said, in answer to his question. 'I
should never have come here.'

'Why?' Matthew moved further into the room, glancing round at the icon-hung walls, and digging the toe of
his expensive loafers into the thick carpet. 'Don't you like
it?'

Samantha made a face. 'No,' she said, not altogether
truthfully. 'I don't like it.'

'But why?' Matthew pushed a hand through his hair,
and allowed it to rest at the back of his neck. The action
parted the lapels of his shirt, a hand-embroidered item
that Samantha guessed must have cost a small fortune,
and compressed the longer hair at the back of his head
against his nape. 'Aren't you comfortable?'

Samantha made a strangled sound. 'Comfortable?' she
echoed. 'I suppose it depends what you mean by comfortable, doesn't it?'

Matthew's dark eyes came to rest on her agitated features. 'I don't understand.' He frowned. 'Has someone
said something to you?'

'No.' Samantha wrapped her arms across her body, and pressed her palms against her elbows. 'No,' she repeated, turning away from his disturbing presence, and moving towards the open doors again. 'I haven't spoken to anyone. I don't speak Greek, do I?'

She sensed him crossing the width of the room to stand beside her, but she held her ground, even if the urge to widen the gap again was strong inside her. They had to have this out, she thought tensely. Even if the idea of arguing with him here was somewhat reckless.

'And that's what's wrong?' he asked, his attractively hoarse voice only inches from her ear. He ran two fingers down her flushed cheek. 'You think it's important that you don't speak the language?'

'Oh, stop it!' Samantha could bear it no longer. Dashing his hand away from her face, she smeared her fingers over the spot. 'Of course that's not what's the matter, and you know it. For heaven's sake, what do you think I am? Don't you think I have any feelings? Oh— probably not. I'm only a—a *waitress*, after all!'

'Hey!' His hand on her shoulder was warm and possessive. It sent a wave of longing surging through her body that she couldn't even begin to deny. 'Don't be angry because I didn't tell you the whole truth——'

'The *whole* truth!' She didn't let him finish, but whirled away from him, grasping the still warm frame of the french door, and gazing at him with wild, impassioned eyes. 'The whole truth! I doubt if anything you've said to me bears the slightest resemblance to the truth!'

Matthew exhaled slowly. 'You don't like this place,' he said mildly. 'Well, I have to admit, it is a little over the top——'

'I don't care about this place!' Samantha fairly yelled at him, and then, aware that her voice was probably audible from other parts of the villa, she toned it down. 'Stop pretending you don't know what I'm talking about. You let me think you worked for a computer company——'

'I do.'

'——when all the time——' His words suddenly diverted her. 'What do you mean, you do?'

'I mean I do work for a computer software company.'

Samantha looked suspicious. 'But you don't have to.'

'Oh, I do. If the company fails, I'll lose all my money.'

'All your money!' Samantha's expression was cynical. 'And I'm expected to believe that?'

'It's true.'

She shook her head. 'So who owns this place?'

'My grandfather.'

'And what does your grandfather do?'

'What does he——' Matthew broke off abruptly, and lifted his shoulders. 'You don't know,' he murmured, after a moment. And then, 'No. How could you?' He made a rueful sound. 'Well, he—he——'

It was the first time she had seen Matthew at a loss for words, and suddenly it all made sense. 'Apollonius!' she exclaimed. 'It was on the helicopter. The Apollonius Corporation! Of course. Your grandfather must be— what was the name?—Aristotle? Yes, that's right. Aristotle Apollonius. My God!' She paled. 'Am I right? Is that who your grandfather is? Aristotle Apollonius!'

Matthew's expression was enough, and she clung to the wooden frame now for support. All the time she had been here, fretting over Matthew's reasons for deceiving her like this, she had never once given a moment's thought to his grandfather's identity. But now she had, and the revelation was mortifying.

'So now you know,' he said, and there was a curiously flat note to his voice. 'Does it make a difference?'

'Does it make a difference?' Samantha gasped. 'Of course it makes a difference!' She quivered. 'How could you even imagine it wouldn't?'

'No.' Matthew shrugged. 'I suppose you're right.'

'You suppose I'm right.' She kept repeating everything he said, but she couldn't seem to help herself. 'Good lord, don't you understand? I came here because I thought—oh, never mind what I thought. I came here believing you were just—just an ordinary person. Not so different from me. A little better off, perhaps. But nothing outrageous. And now—now I find that you're—Aristotle Apollonius's grandson! You're probably going to own this place one day. And—and everything else!'

Matthew's face was sombre. 'And that matters to you?'

Samantha blinked. 'Of course it matters to me. What do you take me for?'

'What do *I* take *you* for?' Now it was Matthew's turn to play mimic. 'I'm afraid I don't understand.'

'Don't you?' Samantha's lips twisted. 'Well, let me put it in words of one syllable for you. I am not your whore! I am not for sale! You can't buy me like you can buy anything else you want, Kyria Putnam!'

'*Kirie*. It's *kirie*,' Matthew corrected automatically, but his eyes were dark and wary. 'Sam——'

'Don't speak to me!' she choked, and now, because this whole interview had taken so much out of her, she was near to tears. 'Just—just find a way to get me out of here. Tonight. Tomorrow. As soon as possible.'

Matthew shook his head. 'You want to leave?'

He seemed astounded at the notion, and she wondered if she was going mad, and that she hadn't said any

of the things she thought she just had. 'Yes,' she told him
unsteadily. 'I want to leave. What did you expect? That
finding out who you really were might persuade me to
forgive you?'

Matthew gazed at her half disbelievingly. 'Let me get
this straight,' he said, and she closed her eyes for a moment, wondering how much more she could take. 'You're
not—impressed by this place.'

'I'm not impressed by *you*!' retorted Samantha, glar-
ing at him. 'Of course I'm impressed by the house. Who
wouldn't be? It's—it's beautiful! But it's not the house
we're talking about, is it? It's you. And—and the lies
you've told to get me here!'

Matthew looked bemused now. 'You're angry,' he said
wonderingly, and Samantha wondered what she had to
do to prove it decisively to him. 'God,' he added, with
more assurance. 'You really are angry.'

'Of course I'm angry!' she exclaimed, her brows
drawing together in sudden confusion when an unexpected smile tipped the corners of his mouth. She
clenched her fists. 'I'm glad you think it's funny.'

'I don't think it's funny,' he replied abruptly, sobering.
But the smile still lurked in the corners of his eyes, and
she didn't altogether believe him. He moved his shoulders in a negligent gesture, and moved closer. 'You never
fail to surprise me, Sam. That's what I like about you.'

Samantha stiffened. The change in his tone was unmistakable, and when he put out his hand, and captured
one of hers, she was hardly surprised at his audacity.

'Is—is that supposed to placate me?' she asked, realising that the only way she could defeat the emotions he
aroused inside her was by hanging on to her anger. 'I
want to go home. And—and if you won't arrange it, I'll
call Paul, and ask him to get me out of here.'

Matthew's mouth flattened. 'Will you?' he said, turning her hand over, in spite of her resistance, and carrying it to his lips. He pressed a kiss on to her palm, and then traced its contours with his tongue. 'And what if I tell you there's no way you can get off this island without my grandfather's permission? The harbour's too small to handle the ferry, and there isn't enough room for a plane to land.'

Samantha's nostrils flared. 'I don't believe you.'

'It's true.' Matthew looked at her through his lashes. 'Would I lie?'

'Yes,' she snapped, snatching her hand away from him. She shook her head. 'Oh—you have no shame, do you? You don't care what happens to me, so long as you get what you want!'

'Forgive me, but I thought it was what you wanted, too,' Matthew ventured, with soft insistence. His eyes drifted down to her mouth. 'And so far as that's concerned, nothing's changed.'

'You're crazy!' It was like knocking her head against a brick wall. 'Haven't you listened to anything I've said?'

'Yes, I've listened.' His eyes dropped to the toes of his loafers. 'You resent the fact that I haven't been entirely honest with you about my background.' He lifted his shoulders in a dismissing gesture, and Samantha, who had been diverted by his apparent submission, suddenly found herself cornered, with the wall of windows on one side, and his arm on the other. 'So—I'm sorry.'

'*Sorry*?'

It was little more than a squeak, with the draught of his breathing shifting the moist hair on her forehead. He was too close, too disturbing, not touching her physically yet, but surrounding her with his warm male presence. Everything about him spelled temptation, and danger, and she knew if she had any sense she'd fight him tooth and nail.

The trouble was that her emotions got in the way of common sense. After living for twenty-four years believing herself capable of handling any situation, *any man*, she was discovering a part of herself she couldn't control. Although she knew he had lied to her before, and would probably lie to her again, he aroused feelings she'd hardly begun to understand, and even without touching her he could turn her bones to water.

'Yes, sorry,' he repeated now, sliding his hand into her hair, and cradling her scalp against his palm. He bent and licked her upper lip with his tongue. 'You're not going to spoil our weekend together just because I wasn't entirely honest about the party?'

Samantha's heart was hammering in her chest. She felt hot, and excited, but frightened as well. Frightened of what he was doing to her, frightened of what she was getting into. Something inside her was telling her that if she let Matthew make love to her there would be no turning back. It was an irrevocable step, and one she would probably live to regret. And yet...

'I—don't know——'

Her words were weak, helpless. *Fool*! *Fool*! The inner warning voice sounded so loud in her ears, she was amazed Matthew couldn't hear it. But evidently he couldn't, because his other hand moved to trap her face, and his thumb brushed sensuously over the lower lip.

'Please,' he said, and the husky tenor of his voice was incredibly persuasive. 'Please.' He lowered his head, and covered her mouth with his. 'Please me,' he begged, against her lips, and his tongue slipped into her mouth.

His arms went round her, his hands sliding down the curve of her spine to her hips. He pulled her against him, against the lean male strength of his body, and between the muscular power of his legs. He held her firmly, inescapably, inflaming her with his heat. Every inch of her body was sensitised by his nearness, and the urgency of his caresses left her no room to think.

He kissed her many times, over and over, possessing her mouth, bruising her mouth, inspiring a burning need that wouldn't be denied. Time lost all meaning as he plundered the vulnerable sweetness of her lips, and although Samantha had begun by resisting his invasion her senses were soon spinning out of reach.

That was when she began to kiss him back, when instincts she had barely grazed with Paul began to take control. She wanted to touch him as he was touching her. She wanted to feel the delight of his skin against hers. Her hands slid up to his neck, and she coiled her fingers in the silky smooth hair at his nape. Then her hands invaded his collar, and she spread her palms against the brown flesh of his shoulders.

'Sam, Sam,' he whispered raggedly, tipping one strap of the vest off her shoulder, and running his teeth across the narrow bones he found there. Then, with a slightly unsteady finger, he traced a line from just below her jaw to the dusky hollow between her breasts. 'So responsive,' he muttered, as her swollen nipples surged against his shirt. And, with an impatient gesture, he tore open his shirt, and brought her even closer. 'I wanted to see you like this. You have such a beautiful body.'

'M-me?' she stammered, gazing up at him, and he deliberately cupped her breast, and crushed the taut bud against his palm.

'You,' he said, averting his eyes. 'Look—have you ever seen anything more beautiful than this?'

She had to look, even though the idea of admiring her own body was as alien to her as the wicked shamelessness of her responses. And, as she watched, he tugged the vest off her shoulders, and allowed his exploring fingers to slide over both naked breasts.

'No bra?' he teased, and her face flamed intolerably.

'I—I didn't bring a strapless one with me,' she protested, but he wasn't listening to her excuses. Instead, he had bent his head towards her and took one exposed nipple into his mouth, suckling on it insistently before transferring his attention to the other.

Samantha's knees almost gave way, and there was an ache in the pit of her stomach. But it wasn't an unpleasant ache. It was an expanding sensation of weakness that spread right through her abdomen, and down into the quivering muscles of her thighs. And with it came a sense of guilt for what she was doing. How could she allow Matthew to caress her in this way, when she had always denied Paul such intimacies?

But coherent thought ceased when he found her mouth again. With his tongue stroking hers, and the unmistakable evidence of his own arousal pressing against her stomach, she felt her senses swimming. Matthew had backed her against the wall, holding her there with his body, so that his hands were free to slide sensuously over her hips and her waist, to the moist underside of her breasts. His thumbs brushed the nipples, still wet and aching from the roughness of his abrasion, and then moved on to her ears, and the sensitive skin just beneath.

'I want you,' he said, against her neck. 'I want to bury myself inside you, and make love to you until you're senseless.'

'Do you?'

It was all she could say, and even that was barely audible. She had never been in such a state before. Never acted this way; never felt this way; never known what it was like to lose control. With the blood drumming in her ears, and all her pre-conceived ideas of her own needs shot to pieces, she was dazed and submissive.

'Yes,' he breathed, his hands cupping her bottom, and bringing her into intimate contact with his swollen manhood. His breath escaped him in a slightly unsteady rush. 'God! You make me feel like a sex-hungry adolescent!'

'Do I?'

Her response was no less unintelligent than before, but with Matthew's lips covering her uptilted face with dozens of hot, eager kisses, and his fingers gripping the backs of her thighs, she was incapable of rational thought. She was drowning; melting in the heat of his arousal; and the only reality was in the demanding pressure of his mouth.

But then, when her scattered senses were crying out for him to take her to the bed, and finish what he had started, he gently, but firmly, pulled away from her. While she gazed at him with uncomprehending eyes, he ran a possessive finger from the waistband of her cotton trousers to the cleft between her legs. But, although his expression was decidedly sensual, his withdrawal was unequivocal.

'You do,' he said, and it took her a moment to realise he was answering her. 'However, even adolescents have to show some restraint.' His lips twisted, and although she sensed it took an effort he turned away from her. 'We're expected to join the family for afternoon tea. A habit my mother acquired when she was married to my father.'

Samantha let her breath out on a gasp, and, hearing her, Matthew paused. Half turning towards her, he took in the wanton picture she made, still resting against the wall of glass, and for a moment he impaled her with his stare.

'Get dressed,' he said tautly, and although Samantha's hands automatically groped for the vest that was balled about her waist her eyes registered the blatant proof that he was still as incapable of controlling his body as she was.

'I—don't know what I'm supposed to wear,' she protested, drawing the crumpled vest against her breasts, and he closed his eyes for a moment, as if he was in pain.

'Right,' he said, after a moment, tugging at the material that was compressing his groin. 'I'll see to it.' And without even a backward glance he walked away from her.

CHAPTER EIGHT

MATTHEW was on his second Scotch when Samantha appeared. Despite his mother's disapproval, he had eschewed tea in favour of something more fortifying, but he was still stunned by his reaction when Samantha walked out on to the terrace.

She looked stunning. He had to admit it. In the knee-length silk shorts and matching halter he had rifled from his mother's wardrobe, she had acquired a surface sophistication that was at once unexpected and appealing. The outfit was mainly turquoise in colour, with exotic streaks of green and blue that shone iridescently when they caught the rays of the dying sun. Combined with her honey-coloured hair and pale skin, the clothes accentuated a latent sensuality, and with gold rings hanging from her ears she was disturbingly unfamiliar.

Yet, when she caught his gaze, he saw at once the uncertainty in her eyes. She might look sophisticated, but she wasn't, and he knew the almost overwhelming urge to stake his possession.

But the maid who had escorted Samantha from her room was intercepted by his mother, and it was Caroline who took narrow-eyed stock of her unwanted house guest. His mother, who had so many clothes she wouldn't recognise them all, was probably wondering how someone in Samantha's position could afford a designer playsuit, Matthew reflected drily, but he returned Caroline's stare with innocent enquiry when she cast an accusing glance in his direction.

There were perhaps thirty people in various stages of relaxation on the terrace. Although his grandfather had had no other children after Matthew's mother, his own siblings had been far more prolific. In consequence, any family gathering was bound to be extensive, with great-aunts and uncles, all eager to enjoy the famous Apollonius hospitality.

Which meant Matthew had to be patient while his mother introduced their guest to the other members of his family. Of course, he could have intervened, and exposed his interest, but he didn't. In spite of his initial reaction to her appearance, he refused to admit his attraction towards her was anything more than a novelty. All the same, he couldn't deny the sense of irritation he felt when one or other of his cousins appeared captivated by her modest smile and lissom figure. He hadn't brought her here to be ogled by his Greek relations, he thought resentfully. He hadn't lent her his mother's clothes so that some other man—most notably his second cousin, Alex—would find her quite so unmistakably to his taste.

But, because he had determined not to display his preference, he was obliged to stay on the sidelines nursing his grievances. And it wasn't until his grandfather came to join him by the drinks trolley that he became aware his attitude had not gone unnoticed.

'So that is the famous Miss Maxwell,' remarked Aristotle Apollonius drily, in his own tongue. 'I must say, she is not what I expected.'

Matthew's brows arched, but that was the only sign he gave that his grandfather's words interested him. 'Really?' he responded politely, picking up the decanter of fine malt whisky and pouring another generous measure into his glass. He glanced at the old man. 'Do you want to join me?'

'In abusing my liver and addling my brain? I don't think so.' Aristotle shook his head disparagingly. 'I shall have one small ouzo before the evening meal. Aside from that, I prefer to keep my wits about me.'

Matthew acknowledged the subtle reproof with a sardonic smile. 'As you say, Papa,' he essayed, adding more ice to his glass, and raising it to his lips. He took a mouthful, and deliberately savoured its texture. 'At your age it's important to preserve your health.'

'And at yours, boy, and at yours,' retorted the old man harshly, his temperament less capable of control than his grandson's. 'For pity's sake, Matthew, why do you persist in provoking me? Do you want to see me dead?'

Matthew's mouth tightened. 'Don't exaggerate, Papa. How I choose to mess up my life is my concern, not yours.'

'I disagree.' The old man squared his shoulders, annoyed as always that Matthew's height gave him the advantage. 'You know what is expected of you. You know that both your mother and myself want to see you married; settled. The whole future of this family rests with you, Matthew. Yet you persist in making gestures which you know will give us pain.'

Matthew kept his temper with a supreme effort. 'And what would you have me do, Papa?' he enquired silkily, watching Samantha as she responded laughingly to something one of his uncles had said. For someone who didn't speak their language, she appeared to be having great success in making herself understood. The knowledge both vexed and aggravated him, and his mood was not improved by his grandfather's persistent recital of an old refrain.

'You should have married Melissa Mainwaring when you had the chance,' declared Aristotle shortly. 'You purported to love her. God knows, you have taken her rejection badly enough! This is why you are standing here, drowning your sorrows in alcohol, is it not? Instead of dancing attendance on that young woman your mother is showing so much interest in.'

Matthew's fingers clenched around his glass. He resented his grandfather's interference in his affairs. It was always the same. Whenever he came here, the old man always treated him as if he were still a boy. But, although he lifted the glass to his lips again, he put it down without drinking. Not because of the truth of what his grandfather had said, but rather because he knew the old man couldn't have been more wrong.

His lips compressed as he realised it was days since he had thought of Melissa with any sense of anguish. The raw bitterness he had lived with since she told him they were through was gone. Oh, he still felt aggrieved and resentful. But that was just his pride reasserting itself.

'What did you say she did for a living?' Aristotle was asking now, and Matthew forced himself to answer the old man civilly.

'Sam?' he queried, watching her progress towards him with increased awareness, and his grandfather sighed.

'Who else? I do not remember Miss Mainwaring having an occupation.'

'No.' Matthew was finding it difficult to concentrate on what his grandfather was saying, and absorb the freedom his contemptuous words had given him. 'No. Melissa enjoys being a lady of leisure. That's why she's marrying Ivanov. He's wealthy enough to give it to her.'

'And you were not?' Aristotle was sceptical.

'I didn't say that. But I don't respond well to coercion,' replied Matthew smoothly.

'And Miss—Maxwell? She does not coerce you?'

'No.'

'So, what does she expect of you?'

'Nothing.' Matthew was abrupt. 'She expects nothing.'

'I find that hard to believe.' His grandfather fixed the young woman in question with a frowning stare. 'Tell me about this—café: is it in need of capital or what?'

'I thought you couldn't remember what she did for a living.' Matthew scowled now. 'But no. So far as I am aware, the café presents no financial problems.'

Aristotle tilted his head. 'So why is she here?'

'Because I invited her,' retorted Matthew. He made another move towards his glass, and then, as if resenting the impulse that had driven him to seek its balm, he thrust his hands into the pockets of his trousers. 'Do you want to meet her?'

'Do you need an excuse to remove her from your mother's protection?' suggested the old man shrewdly, and Matthew gave him a fulminating glare.

'What is that supposed to mean?'

'Why—only that you have been watching her for the past fifteen minutes with undisguised impatience,' responded his grandfather mildly. 'If I did not know better, I would say you were jealous.'

Matthew's jaw clamped. 'But you do know better,' he said, between his teeth. 'And if I appear concerned, perhaps it's because my mother isn't usually known for her benevolence towards outsiders.'

'Hmm.' His grandfather conceded the point. 'And this girl means something to you?'

Matthew stiffened. 'Not in the way you mean, old man,' he answered, disliking his own unguarded reaction to the idea. Just for a moment, his senses had leapt, and then a brooding sense of foreboding swept over him. However, he brushed such thoughts aside in his eagerness to forestall his grandfather. He decided it was easier to foster the belief that he was still fretting over Melissa's departure than to admit Samantha had any—albeit transient—hold on his affections. 'She intrigues me because she's so independent,' he said, adopting a determinedly careless tone. 'And Melissa deserves a little taste of her own medicine.'

'So—you are using this young woman to effect some—revenge?' Aristotle sounded appalled, and Matthew sighed.

'Not entirely,' he admitted, unable to maintain that, even to himself. 'But, our association is—purely—sexual.' His mouth tightened again as a spasm of pure physical need scorched through him. And, to divert his grandfather's attention from any further introspection, he added, 'I need a woman, Papa. Surely you haven't forgotten how that feels?'

'No.' Aristotle emitted a rueful sound. 'No, I have not forgotten the demands of the flesh. But beware of imitations, Matthew. There is an old proverb that says the man who lights the fire is not immune from being burned.'

Matthew offered a faint smile, but he made no comment. In all honesty, it was taking all his powers of restraint to remain where he was. For, although Samantha's introduction to the other members of his family was now complete, his mother was making sure she didn't interrupt his conversation with his grandfather.

It angered, and infuriated him. And he was damn sure his grandfather was aware of it. Had they concocted this between them? he wondered with a rare flash of self-persecution. My God! He was getting neurotic! The sooner he got what he wanted from Samantha and sent her packing, the better it would be for all of them.

And, to expedite this decision, he took a deep breath, and said, 'If you'll excuse me, Papa,' before striding purposefully towards his objective. He no longer cared that he was showing his hand. It mattered little to him what his relatives, distant or otherwise, might think of his behaviour. Threading his way between chairs and lounges, and gaily striped couches, he made his way towards Samantha without deviating, the words he exchanged in passing barely civil in their brevity.

She saw him coming. In spite of the fact that she was having tea with his uncle Henry, she seemed to sense his relentless approach. Of course, his mother noticed it, too, but she was far more adept at hiding her feelings. And Henry, who was once again playing truant from Aunt Celia's many illnesses, was the obvious choice of companion, as he was English, too.

And it was Henry who greeted his nephew with his usual aplomb. 'Getting your usual lecture from the old man, Matt?' he asked, after the usual courtesies had been exchanged, and Caroline Putnam gave him a glowering look.

'No doubt Apollo was only saying how delighted he was that Matthew's here,' she retorted, as her son placed a proprietorial hand on Samantha's shoulder.

'And the rest,' jeered Henry irrepressibly. 'Anyone who likes to be called Apollo has to have a fairly high opinion of themselves. And we all know what the old man expects of his grandson.'

'I notice you don't turn down his invitations!' exclaimed Caroline hotly, torn between her desire to defend her father, and the knowledge that by excluding Matthew and Samantha from the conversation she was running the risk of losing her advantage. 'Matt——' She caught his arm as he would have turned away. 'Aren't you going to introduce Samantha to your grandfather?'

'Later,' said Matthew flatly, in no mood to have another run-in with Aristotle. He glanced round, and saw to his relief that his grandfather had been joined by several other members of the family. 'He's busy right now,' he added, feeling Samantha's resistance as he endeavoured to guide her away. 'You don't mind if we go for a walk, do you? I'd like to show Samantha the caves.'

'Oh, well——' Caroline was evidently casting about in her mind for some reason why he ought not to leave the party, but Matthew was not prepared to humour her either.

'*Herete*,' he said, using the Greek farewell deliberately. And before his mother could say anything else he urged Samantha across the terrace.

'You might have asked me if I wanted to go for a walk,' she hissed, as they reached the shallow steps that led down to the beach. 'I may be here because you brought me, but I do have feelings, you know.'

'I know.' Matthew offered his hand as she descended the steps and scowled when she refused it. 'But we couldn't have had a private conversation with my mother around. What did you think of her, by the way? What did she say to you?'

Samantha's expression was not encouraging. He could tell she was uneasy at being removed from the comparative security of being with other people, and he guessed she had had second thoughts about what had happened earlier that afternoon.

'Your—your mother was very nice,' she replied now, taking off her shoes, and carrying them suspended from one hand. 'She asked me how long I'd known you.'

Matthew glanced sideways at her. 'And what did you say?'

'I said, not long,' she replied shortly, turning aside from his dogged trek along the beach, and heading for the water. She was evidently aware that by doing so she remained within sight of the terrace, and Matthew stifled his impatience as he kicked off his shoes and joined her.

She was already paddling in the shallows, gasping when a wave more aggressive than the others splashed foam about her calves. She looked up when he joined her, but her eyes were dark and wary. It was obvious she wasn't happy, and he was irritated by his concern.

'So what else did she say?' he persisted, treading into the shallows, and she gave him a shocked stare.

'You're getting your trousers wet!' she exclaimed, pointing at the water lapping round his ankles, but Matthew only moved nearer.

'I'll take them off, if you like,' he said, feeling a certain malicious satisfaction when her face bloomed with colour. 'Come on, Sam. Don't shut me out. I thought we agreed to call a truce for this weekend.'

The tip of her tongue appeared, and Matthew wondered how such a simple gesture could affect him so. 'I—I don't remember anything about a truce,' she said, looking down at the specks of water that dappled her shorts. 'You didn't even tell me what I was supposed to do after I got changed.'

Matthew frowned. 'Didn't Rosita wait for you?'

'The maid?' Samantha shrugged. 'Yes, I suppose so. But you must have known how I'd feel, meeting all these people! And—and instead of being there, you let your mother——'

'My mother got to you before I could,' he retorted, taking a wind-blown strand of her hair between his thumb and forefinger, and smoothing it tensely. 'Sam, believe me, I wanted to be with you. But sometimes it's better to let events take their course.'

She looked up. 'Was your grandfather talking about me?'

Matthew hesitated. 'Among other things.'

'He doesn't like you bringing me here, does he?' Her lips twisted. 'I don't think your mother's too overjoyed about it either.'

'Why?' Matthew stepped nearer, so that the rippling waves had only a narrow channel between their feet. 'If she said anything to upset you——'

'She didn't.' Samantha broke in before he could voice the fury he was feeling. 'I—just got the impression that— well, that she was warning me off, that's all. She implied I shouldn't take you too seriously.'

'Did she?' In spite of the fact that only a short time before he had been telling himself much the same thing, Matthew felt a wave of raw resentment sweep over him. How dared his mother presume on their relationship? And what the hell did she know of his feelings, when they only saw one another perhaps a dozen times a year?

'It doesn't matter.' Samantha put up a hand and removed her hair from his fingers, before turning away. 'Oh, look—isn't that a pretty shell? When I was young I used to collect shells, and make them into bracelets.'

Matthew exhaled heavily. 'And did you tell her how we met?' he persisted, moving up behind her, and sliding his arms around her waist. To hell with the fact that anyone who chose could watch them from the terrace. He needed to touch her, and the warmth of her slim hips was heaven against his tortured body.

'Matt!' Her protest was half-hearted, but she, much more than he, was conscious of their audience. 'Your mother can see us,' she added, as he brushed her hair aside, and kissed the soft skin at the nape of her neck. 'Oh—please, Matt! You can't do this. What will your grandfather think of us?'

'He'll think I'm a very lucky man,' muttered Matthew huskily, turning, so that she was hidden by his lean frame. Then his fingers spread possessively over the burgeoning fullness of her breasts. 'Mmm, baby, can you feel what you do to me?'

'You mustn't!'

Her denial was breathless, and automatic, but for all her words she was leaning into him, yielding against his arousal that swelled unmistakably against her rounded bottom. Like him, she was responding to the flame of pure desire that swept between them, and his words were barely audible against the hollow of her ear.

'Come and see the caves,' he breathed, twisting her round in his arms, and gazing down into her wide, anxious eyes. 'At least no one will see us there.'

Samantha swallowed. Matthew watched the nervous contraction of her throat, and was amazed at the proprietorial feeling he felt towards her. She belonged to him, he thought irrationally; not her fiancé, Paul, whoever he might be. He'd decide when he'd let her go. And it might not be as soon as he'd thought.

'I—all right,' she gave in huskily, and for a moment Matthew was tempted to kiss her there, in full view of anyone who cared to look. But discretion—and the

awareness of his own ungovernable impulses, so far as
she was concerned—persuaded him to be patient, and,
turning her beneath the arch of his arm, he drew her
more familiarly along the shoreline.

The caves stretched for some distance around the curve
of the headland. A labyrinthine warren of caverns and
tunnels, they had once been the haunt of pirates and
thieves. In the early part of the nineteenth century, they
had also been used as shelter, by the peasants fleeing from
the Sultan's men. It was said that thousands of men and
women had been shipped to Constantinople, and sold
into slavery.

Happily, nowadays, the only occupants were crabs and
seabirds. The smooth, sandy floors were strewn with
seaweed, not kegs of rum, and the arched roofs only
echoed to the sound of the ocean.

Matthew's intention, of taking Samantha into his arms
the minute they were out of sight of prying eyes, was diverted by her reaction to the caves. She was enchanted by
the realisation that there were several entrances to the
caverns, and her delight at discovering they could walk
under the headland, and emerge on to another beach that
had no other means of access, was infectious. He found
himself sharing her search for shells, and admiring the
veined bones of marble that pushed through the cliff-
face. He even shared her laughter when a hermit-crab
appeared from behind a rock, and threatened to nip her
toes.

She was unaffected, and amusing, and Matthew
couldn't help responding to her natural charm. It wasn't
just that he wanted to make love to her. Though he did,
more and more, he reflected ruefully. It was simply that
she was marvellous fun to be with, and he found himself
in the unexpected position of wanting her all to himself.

The knowledge didn't please him. He was allowing the demands of his libido to influence his reasoning, he thought irritably. He wanted to have sex with her, that was all. Once he had satisfied his physical needs, the other characteristics about her that he admired would all fall into perspective.

But what if they didn't? a small voice argued. What if, by making love to her, he only opened the gates to a deeper involvement? After his relationship with Melissa, how could he even contemplate the traumas of another affair?

He couldn't, he decided abruptly. This whole situation was getting dangerously out of hand. His mother and grandfather were right. He shouldn't have brought Samantha here.

He glanced at his watch. It was after five. The gathering on the terrace would have broken up by now, everyone retiring to their own apartments, to rest for a while before changing for dinner. It was a very leisurely life they led here on Delphus. There was far too much time to dwell on other things.

His jaw tightened as he turned to look at Samantha. She was squatting down by a rock-pool, chasing a tiny nautilus shell with her finger. The position she had adopted drew his attention to the provocative curve of hip and thigh, and the dipping of her neckline exposed the creamy-soft roundness of one perfect breast.

His hands clenched. What he wanted to do at that moment was tumble her on to the sand and kiss her senseless. But instead he looked away, and said in a voice that couldn't help but reveal his tension, 'Shall we go?'

'Go?' Samantha came to her feet in one fluid motion, and her eyes were an unknowing mirror to the confusion of her thoughts. 'I—why, yes.' She glanced around her. 'Can we come here again?'

'If you like.' Matthew was offhand, but he couldn't help it, and, pushing his hands into his pockets, he walked back the way they had come.

She followed him, but he sensed she was as disturbed as he was by the sudden darkening of his mood. It was crazy, he told himself angrily. His emotions weren't involved here; only his senses. So why was he acting like a moron, when she was his for the taking?

He was relieved to see that the terrace was practically deserted when they reached it. Only a handful of servants were bustling about, clearing the remains of the tea-party, and stacking the chairs for the night. They smiled politely at Matthew, but he guessed his and Samantha's prolonged absence had been commented upon. He had probably been judged, and found guilty, of every sin in the book, he reflected bitterly. Greeks respected their women; they didn't take advantage of them.

'Do you know the way to your rooms?' Matthew asked as they entered the wide entrance hall that was flooded now with the golden light of early evening. He was already contemplating the prospect of the decanter of Scotch his grandfather kept in the library with some desperation, and his heart thudded heavily when Samantha shook her head.

'I'm sorry, no.'

She looked—anxious; hurt! Those eyes, that he had once pictured dark with passion, possessed a troubled expression. He wasn't totally convinced of it, but he suspected she was on the verge of tears. Dear God! he thought despairingly. What was he going to do?

Keeping his hands securely in his pockets, he managed a casual, 'OK.'

But her, 'I'll ask one of the maids to direct me,' stung him to the core.

'Don't be silly,' he retorted, setting off along the corridor to their right. 'Come on. I'll show you how to find your way. Then—then when it's dinnertime, you won't need anyone's assistance.'

Samantha sighed. He heard the soft expellation of her breath behind him, but he didn't look back. And presently she fell into step beside him, probably aware that, by dragging her heels, she was only prolonging the situation.

It was shadowy in the long corridors, the lamps that cast their illumination by night not yet reaching their full potential. Instead, the brass-shaded lanterns cast pools of shadow over the rug-strewn floors, and Matthew hoped fervently that Samantha wouldn't lose her footing. He didn't know what he might do if he had to touch her. Every inch of his skin was sensitised to every move she made.

But Samantha didn't slip, and they reached her door without incident. Set in an angle of the corridor, its grilled panels had never appeared so welcome, and Matthew managed a grim smile as he indicated that they had arrived.

'Dinner's not until nine o'clock,' he said, keeping the vision of his grandfather's decanter firmly in his sights. 'If you have any difficulties in finding your way, just pick up the phone.'

Samantha nodded. She hadn't bothered putting her shoes on again since they re-entered the house, and in consequence the difference in their height was more pronounced. But, when she tilted her head and looked up at him, she had no problem in meeting his gaze.

'Is something wrong?' she asked softly, and Matthew's breathing stilled.

'I'm afraid I——'

He wasn't sure what he had been about to say, but in any case he wasn't allowed to continue. 'Did I do something wrong?' she queried, putting out her hand and touching his taut chest. Her fingers brushed the fine dark hair exposed by the opening of his shirt, and he shuddered. 'You know what I'm talking about. You've hardly said a word for the last half-hour.'

Matthew sucked in a laboured breath. 'You're imagining things.'

'No, I'm not.' Amazingly, she seemed prepared to stand and argue with him. Her face, pale in the artificial light, took on a shuttered look. 'I think you're having second thoughts about bringing me here——'

'No!' Matthew's hard-won restraint faltered, but he made a valiant effort to keep his head. 'No, I—just think we both need a breathing space, that's all. I've been doing some—thinking, and I guess what I'm saying is—that——'

'—you wish you hadn't brought me here!' she finished tensely, and, stepping round his astounded frame, she marched into her apartment.

Matthew saw the door closing behind her, swung by the aggressive sweep of her arm, and somehow his foot prevented it from slamming. 'For pity's sake, Sam!' he exclaimed, striding after her, and it was not until he had caught her arm, and jerked her round to face him, that he realised how reckless he had been.

She was crying. The tears he had suspected earlier were now a reality, overspilling her eyes in the aftermath of their encounter. Salty streaks smeared her cheeks, and she smudged them away with the back of her hand, as she struggled to meet his angry gaze.

'Oh, God!'

The oath he muttered was as much a prayer for his own deliverance as a protest at her vulnerability. But it was impossible for him to look at her without touching her, and when he pulled her into his arms he felt only relief.

'I'm sorry,' he muttered harshly, chasing her tears with his tongue, before finding the parted softness of her mouth. 'I never meant to hurt you, and what I've done has hurt us both.'

The sound she made could have been a protest, but her hands were gripping the hair at the back of his neck, and she was reaching up eagerly towards him. So much so that Matthew's tongue brushed the dewy softness at the back of her throat, and her eyes closed against the passion she saw in his.

She felt so good in his arms, he thought unsteadily, her shoulders warm from the unaccustomed rays of the sun. Her skin felt like satin, and when he insinuated one hand into the waistband of her shorts he was amazed at the sense of power it gave him.

He wanted her! Lord, how he wanted her! He had never felt such a need to be a part of a woman before, and the hunger she inspired in him made a nonsense of his resistance. What was the point of sending her away? He knew that if he did sooner or later he'd go after her. He wouldn't rest until she was his, and to hell with the consequences.

She was kissing him back now, her tongue seeking his in an eager parody of his possession. Her body was leaning into his, and the unmistakable scent of her arousal rocked his senses. Whatever kind of relationship she had with her fiancé, he was convinced she had never responded like this before. It was crazy, but for all her eagerness to taste his mouth there was an immaturity in the way she went about it. Instinct alone seemed to be responsible for the wilful urgency of her lips, and although she must have some experience there was a guileless naïveté in the way she let him take the lead.

The curve of her bottom was like the softest silk beneath his hand. His fingers cupped it, squeezed it, used it to urge her even nearer, revelling in the expectation of that soft skin against his own.

Eagerness was making him reckless. He hardly remembered that while he had been escorting her to her room he had been steeling himself against her. His earlier plans of spending the evening in a sensual anticipation of the night ahead; of watching her across the supper table, and teasing his senses with thoughts of her eventual acquiescence, had all been discarded. The idea of savouring her submission, of picturing her slim body, pale against his crisp sheets, had become too dangerous to contemplate. Yet, suddenly, even those images seemed too distant to withstand.

He wanted her now; this minute. Holding her like this, feeling her yielding body responding to the urgency of his, made even his pre-conceived seduction superfluous. Far from tempting her, she was tempting him, driving him to distraction with her bewitching innocence.

His hand groped for the door behind him, and he slammed it shut. Then, keeping his mouth on hers, he urged her back, towards the bed. The swagged edge of the counterpane halted their progress, and Samantha sat down rather suddenly, jerked out of her bemusement by the coolness against her legs.

Realising it might not be wise to give himself time to rekindle any doubts about what he was doing, Matthew dropped on to his haunches in front of her. He moved between her splayed knees, and cupped her face in his hands, parting her lips with his thumbs, and slipping his tongue between.

'Matt...'

His name on her lips was dazed and questioning, but there was no trace of resistance in the word. On the contrary, as his fingers moved to stroke down the column of her throat, she shifted against him, brushing his hand with her breasts as a whispering sigh rippled over her.

Matthew found he was trembling. The gentle hands that probed his shoulders were unknowingly sensuous, and his whole body yearned for their delicate caress. He could feel his muscles stirring, growing and expanding, and the ache between his thighs was becoming unbearable.

He found the ends of the cords that kept the halter in place, and tugged decisively. The two sides parted, and the silk fell away. Her breasts were just as beautiful as he remembered, and he pressed his face between them, reaching behind her again to unfasten the ties at her waist.

The halter was tossed on to the floor beside him, and her eyes met his half nervously as his hands slid from her waist to cradle the undersides of her breasts. The rose-tipped crests seemed to surge towards him, and she quivered when his teeth closed around one sensitised peak.

He suckled greedily, causing a flood of feeling to torment his groin. He had never experienced such a sensation of excitement; never felt such a rush of adrenalin, spreading through his veins like wildfire. His heart was thumping; the blood was pounding in his head. Every nerve and sinew was demanding satisfaction.

Cool it, Matt, he chided himself, drawing back for a moment and looking down at the floor, trying to calm his rioting senses. But the sight of his own aroused body was unavoidable, and the palpable nearness of hers made a nonsense of his efforts. It was impossible to behave rationally in his present state of upheaval. His brain felt as if it was on fire, and his physical needs were paramount.

His hand moved down, one finger drawing a line from the waistband of her shorts, over her flat stomach, to the heated junction of her legs. She jumped when he pressed his thumb against her, and he felt the throbbing pulse beneath the silk. He couldn't wait to strip the shorts from her. He wanted to touch her without the barrier of anything between.

And yet there was a tantalising delight in prolonging his own torture. He knew that what was going to happen between them would be good, and he wanted her to enjoy it as much as he would. That was why he drew one of her hands to his body, sucking in his breath when her slender fingers traced the turgid outline of his flesh.

She was trembling now, and if he hadn't known better he'd have said she was half afraid of what was happening. But she didn't draw back. In fact, she seemed disarmingly eager to learn anything he had to teach her. And, when her fingers went to release his zip, he decided she still had a lot to learn.

He moved then, tumbling her back on to the bed, and coming down on it beside her. With one hand, he tore open his shirt, so that when he bent over her her breasts were flattened against the hair-roughened skin of his chest, and with the other he cushioned her head, bringing her mouth to his.

It was so good to feel her beneath him, so good to find the button of her shorts and ease them down over her hips. She was wearing lacy briefs beneath, but they were soon disposed of. And then his fingers found the damp sweetness they had been seeking.

'God, Sam,' he muttered, releasing the button of his trousers and jerking open his zip. He almost groaned at the relief he felt when his swollen flesh spilled into his hand. Dear God, he thought incredulously, this had never happened to him before, not even with Melissa. He was as horny as a schoolboy on his first date.

She was shifting beneath him now, and although when his mouth found hers and his tongue plunged deeply into her mouth she responded avidly he sensed her uncertainty. And why not? he asked himself, with a brief spurt of conscience. It was obvious she had never been unfaithful to her boyfriend before. Indeed, if she hadn't been so adamant about her relationship with her fiancé, he might even have suspected she had never done this before.

But he didn't want to think about that. She was too deliciously desirable, and responsive. Her lips, bruised now from his kisses, were a constant delight, and the ripeness of her breasts simply begged for his attention.

His gaze drifted down to her hips and her flat stomach. The curly mound of her womanhood was soft and irresistible, and he slid his fingers into the cleft that was wet with wanting him. Even though he longed to taste her, he knew he dared not risk that right now. His own urgent body demanded release, and he had to content himself with stroking the hot little nub that pulsed against his thumb.

She jerked beneath his touch, and the whimpering sounds she emitted drove him crazy. He wanted her to make those sounds when he was inside her, and, sliding his hand along her thigh, he parted it from the other.

With his tongue tracing the column of her throat, he moved between her legs, and guided himself into that dark moist passage, and when she bucked against him his flagging control gave way.

He entered her swiftly, more swiftly than he had intended, and even when he encountered that unbelievable—but unmistakable—barrier, he couldn't draw back. For the first time in his life, his own needs got the better of him, and, even though he struggled to resist, the marvellous tightness of her muscles defeated him.

He climaxed almost immediately, spilling most of his seed inside her. For, although he dragged himself away from that spiralling ecstasy, the effort had exhausted him, and he slumped heavily beside her . . .

CHAPTER NINE

SAMANTHA stared up at the ceiling. Even in the lamp-light the delicate plasterwork was clearly visible. The flowing style, which gave each leaf and flower such vitality, must have taken a craftsman months to create. Leaves and flowers that had no colour, she reflected tautly. Like everything else at the villa, they weren't exactly what they seemed.

She sighed. She supposed she ought to be feeling bad at this moment. Or guilty, at least, for behaving as she had. If Paul could see her now, he would never forgive her. So why did she just feel empty, and incapable of grief?

She wished Matthew would go. He was still motionless beside her, one arm raised, and his head turned away from her. He was probably still nursing his outrage at finding she was still a virgin. Judging by the oath he had uttered seconds before he had slumped beside her, he was unlikely to forgive her. Join the queue, she thought indifferently. She would probably never forgive herself.

She supposed she was still numb from the experience. Certainly, it had been nothing like what she had expected. It had been more painful, for one thing. But then, remembering the rampant power of Matthew's body, she ought not to have been surprised. No wonder women were afraid of men forcing themselves upon them.

Matthew hadn't done that, but he had hurt her. The blood still caked her thighs with its sticky, cloying scent.

What was harder to understand were the feelings that had swept through her body like a forest fire, and now seemed no more substantial than a mirage. What had happened to them? Why did they seem so unreal? Her ignorance had to be the key; that, and a hopeless sense of inadequacy.

She didn't blame Matthew. The responsibility was all hers. She had gone into this with her eyes open. It was her fault it had turned out the way it had.

He stirred then, and, unable to prevent herself, she stiffened. If he touched her, she would scream, she thought unsteadily. For God's sake, why didn't he just go? How much longer was this to go on?

But Matthew didn't go. Nor did he touch her; not initially, anyway. He merely rolled his head on his arm so that he was looking at her, and she stared at the ceiling with greater concentration.

'Am I supposed to say I'm sorry?' he asked softly, expelling his breath on a low sigh. 'I am. But not for the reason you think. I haven't done this since I was in school.'

In spite of herself, that got her attention. Unable to resist, she turned to look at him, her narrowed eyes mirroring her arrant disbelief. 'Really?'

'Yes, really.' Matthew's eyes were dark and intent. 'I'm usually in control. This time I wasn't. As I say, I'm sorry. I'll make sure it doesn't happen again.'

'Again?' Samantha gasped. 'You surely can't imagine this might happen again?' His shamelessness disturbed her, and she hurriedly looked away. 'I'm not blaming you, but—it was a mistake. I knew it before I came here, and this has only proved the point.'

'Why?' Matthew shifted, so that his weight was supported on one elbow, and he was looking down at her. 'Because you'd never been with a man before?' He ran lazy fingers into his hair, and, seeing the movement out of the corner of her eye, Samantha knew a moment's panic. 'You should have told me. I hurt you, I know. But,' he shrugged, 'it had to happen some time.'

'You would say that, wouldn't you?' Samantha had to catch herself back from saying something quite vituperative about this experience. For a moment a wave of some emotion she refused to recognise swept over her. And she despised herself for being more conscious of his nakedness than her own. 'Well—as I say, I'm not blaming you. I knew what I was doing. I just—didn't think it through.'

The trace of a smile tugged at the corners of Matthew's lips. 'No one thinks this sort of thing through, sweetheart,' he told her gently, and she clenched her fists against the casual endearment. 'And forgive me, I don't believe you did know what you were doing. If it's any consolation, nor did I.'

Samantha refused to be cajoled. Pulling her lower lip between her teeth, she said, 'I think you'd better go. It's getting late. Your—your mother will be wondering where you are.'

Matthew shrugged, his shoulders brown and muscular in the subdued light. 'That's not a consequence that troubles me greatly,' he remarked, his eyes drifting down over her taut body. 'I just wish I'd locked that door. There are some things no one else should see.'

Samantha's head jerked around. 'You don't think——'

'Relax.' His hand came to touch her now, and she hardly noticed the light caress. She was too shocked at the idea that anyone else might see her humiliation. She could just imagine the gossip that would cause.

'Stay there,' he said after a moment, seeming to find it difficult to withdraw his hand from the smooth curve of her arm. But at least he didn't touch her breasts, which were already hardening against her will. Dear God, she thought, as feeling flooded back into her bones, she couldn't want him again; not after what had happened before.

Matthew slid off the bed, and although she wished she could look anywhere else but at him, her eyes followed his unashamed progress to her bathroom. He disappeared inside, and presently she heard water running. For heaven's sake, she wondered, was he taking a shower? Of course! He'd want to clean all trace of their lovemaking from him.

She sat up and looked down at herself, finding no pleasure in the sight. If only there were another bathroom, she thought. If only she could cleanse herself before he came back. Crazy though the thoughts were, she doubted anyone would want to touch her at the moment. Which should have been a source of relief—but wasn't.

Matthew seemed to take forever, and she was on the point of deciding she could at least put on her dressing-gown when he came back. But he hadn't had a shower. His hair was dry, and there was no lingering smell of soap clinging to his body. On the contrary, his skin was still glistening with sweat, and when he came towards the bed she saw he was fully aroused.

'Come on,' he said, and before she could ascertain his intentions he had scooped her up into his arms.

Shock soon gave way to comprehension, when he carried her into the bathroom. Instead of the shower she had thought he was taking, Matthew had filled the enormous tub, and now he paused on the marble rim, looking down into the gently steaming water. Then, just when she thought he was going to lower her into the tub and leave her to her ablutions, he stepped down into the pool by means of the shallow steps cut into the side, and deposited her on the ledge that encircled it below the waterline.

The water was neither hot nor cold, and Samantha felt the instant relief of its soothing balm, pine-scented and luxurious, against her sore body. She realised she really could have swum in its depths, but it was far more sybaritic just to let its heat relax her.

'Good, hmm?' Matthew murmured, and Samantha, who had been too bemused by her surroundings to notice that he was still there, caught her breath.

His presence both shocked and disturbed her. Shocked, because she had never taken a bath with a man before; and disturbed, because she was aware that her attraction towards him had by no means been abated by what had happened.

'I—very good,' she answered him now, suddenly aware of her breasts, clearly outlined beneath the water that lapped about her shoulders. And of the abandoned way she was lounging, also visible to his appraising gaze. 'Um—thank you.'

Dammit, why didn't he go? she wondered frantically. He must know how embarrassing this was for her. She couldn't believe, with his vast experience, he didn't know exactly how she was feeling.

But instead of getting out of the tub he reached for an ivory tablet of soap that was set on a dish to one side of the bath, and applied its softness to the sponge he was squeezing in his other hand. Then, to Samantha's astonishment—and mortification—he began to lather her arms and shoulders.

'I—don't,' she protested, as the sponge made a circle round her breast, and Matthew's lips tilted at her obvious distress.

'Why not?' he asked, ignoring her in any case. 'I'll be very thorough, I assure you.'

'Because—because you can't,' Samantha gasped, her voice rising dramatically as the sponge moved lower. 'Matt—please! You're embarrassing me.'

Matthew's hand stilled. 'Don't be silly,' he said, leaning towards her and circling her lips with his tongue. 'Just pretend I'm your body-slave.' He drew back and grinned. 'I am, anyway.' The sponge slid along her thigh. 'Come on. I won't hurt you. I promise.'

'Oh, Matt!' To her dismay, she felt the stirring heat of the same emotions that had betrayed her once already. It couldn't be true, she told herself. After the fiasco of what had happened, how could she even contemplate making love with him without horror?

'Oh, baby,' he countered softly, drawing her off the ledge and into his arms. 'God, Sam, what are you doing to me?'

What was she doing to him? Samantha could have laughed at the incongruity of it all. What was he doing to her, more like? With the water soothing her aching limbs, the idea of making love again was no longer so painful, and all thoughts of right and wrong fled.

Matthew lifted her out of the bath with the utmost tenderness, wrapping her in a huge silky towel that encased her like a cocoon. Then, uncaring of his own wetness, he laid her on the bed and finished his task.

However, by the time he had attended to her breasts, punctuating the towel's soft abrasion with sensuous kisses, and caressed the calf and instep of each long, shapely leg, she was weak and clinging to him. She no longer cared that his throbbing arousal might hurt her yet again. She just wanted him inside her, hot and fulfilling.

And he was hot: hot, and fulfilling, and marvellously real. There was no pain, just an aching fullness as he stretched her taut muscles, and slid into her sheath. His mouth bruised hers as he withdrew part-way, only to thrust himself inside her again, and a growing sense of anticipation flowered in her stomach.

Instinct took over. She was hardly aware of what she was doing. With Matthew's tongue taking possession of her mouth, mimicking the hard possession of his body, and his hands cupping her bottom to bring her even nearer, she wrapped her legs around his waist, and let him take her. The plunging heat as he drove himself into her was like a mounting wave of pleasure, the slickness of his body welding them together. She moaned out loud as the fiery heat of their lovemaking reached a crescendo, and then a splintering delight engulfed her, sending her spinning over the brink...

Samantha dressed for supper with shaking hands. Although she knew Matthew would be there to support

her, she would have given everything she possessed just
to avoid joining the rest of his family for the evening
meal. She was convinced they would know exactly what
had happened between that too-obvious walk along the
beach, and supper. She was sure they would see
Matthew's mark upon her. And, although the only
bruises she had were hidden by the long skirt of her Laura
Ashley print, she felt so different that she couldn't believe she didn't look different, too.

But different didn't mean like him, she reminded herself tensely. In spite of what had happened—in spite of
the fact that he had turned her world upside-down in the
space of a few hours—Samantha knew that nothing had
really changed. She was still the owner of the Honey Pot
Café, and Matthew was still Aristotle Apollonius's
grandson.

Still? She questioned her use of the adverb. Matthew
wasn't 'still' anything. Until today, she hadn't even realised he owned J.P. Software International. J.P.? She
frowned. P for Putnam, no doubt. If only she had been
more astute. She might have put two and two together
before it was too late.

But it was too late, she acknowledged. Much too late.
Whatever happened in the future, today had been a cru-
cial turning point in her life. It was the day she had
learned now naïve she had been to believe she had control of her life. It was the day she had learned that,
whatever happened now, she would have to tell Paul she
couldn't marry him.

She looked down at her bare finger. Even though she
had only been wearing her engagement ring for a few
weeks, she missed its narrow band. It had represented so
many things to her—home, security, normality! The

common-sense values she had always lived by. Now she realised what a momentous thing she had done when she had taken it off on the plane. She had done more than remove a ring, she thought ominously. She had shed the beliefs of a lifetime.

She drew an uneven breath. So what now? she wondered tautly. Where did she go from here? The common sense that had deserted her when Matthew touched her had now returned with a vengeance. All right, for a few hours he had shown her heaven. But, although she didn't have his experience, she was sensible enough to realise that what he had shared with her he had probably shared with someone else. More than one someone, probably. She had to accept that, no matter how painful that possibility might be.

So where did that leave her? What could she expect from this relationship? At the most, a few weeks of Matthew's time. A brief, if sexually satisfying, affair, with no commitment from either of them? Or would she become another Melissa, using any ruse to see him, even if it meant using another man? For she had the uneasy feeling that Matthew's strange appearance at Melissa's engagement party was less of a coincidence than he had admitted. He had said Melissa had expected to marry *him*! At least Samantha had had no such expectation.

She sighed, and took another look at her appearance. The dress was fine, but she wasn't. She didn't belong here. No matter that only an hour ago she had held Matthew, shuddering in her arms. No matter that, in spite of everything, she was very much afraid she had fallen in love with him. She was only prolonging the agony. He didn't love her. He *wanted* her, that was all. She doubted he had ever really loved anybody. Love—and marriage—were not part of his agenda. They didn't fit in with his plans for the future. So how could she, when her ambitions would always be so different from his?

Half of her wished there were some way she could leave without seeing Matthew again. The prospect of the weekend ahead filled her with alarm. No matter how strong her resolve might be—to break this alliance before it broke her—the longer they were together, the harder it was going to be. She didn't want to get used to being with him. She didn't want him to break her heart.

But the other half, the emotional half of her being, saw the next two days quite differently. Forty-eight hours was a long time, she told herself optimistically. Matthew might even fall in love with her. And, as she couldn't get away, why shouldn't she take what the gods had offered, and be grateful?

Fat chance! she thought, pragmatism overwhelming her illusions. Get real, Sam, she ordered bitterly, dragging a brush savagely through her hair. This was life, not some fancy daydream! And anyway, did she really want to marry a man who saw no shame in seducing another man's fiancée?

She threw down the brush, and turned away from the mirror. It didn't help to see her own culpability in her eyes. Matthew would not have made love to her if she hadn't accepted his invitation. The only person responsible for messing up her life was herself.

The knock at the door brought an abrupt end to her unhappy introspection. And, although moments before she had been torn with indecision, she didn't hesitate before going to answer it. There was nothing she could do, she insisted, when the low insidious voice of reason still protested. When she got back to England, she would tell

Matthew she couldn't see him again. But, until then, she was helpless.

She had locked the door on his departure an hour ago, the defensive action a small sop to her conscience. Which was probably why he hadn't just walked in, she acknowledged drily. After what had happened between them, she couldn't imagine Matthew showing any reticence.

But, when she opened the door, it wasn't Matthew who was standing outside. It was his mother. And Samantha gazed at her blankly, but with a growing sense of dread.

'Samantha.' Caroline Putnam—or did she still call herself Apollonius? Samantha wondered wildly—smiled disarmingly. 'May I come in?'

'I—of course.' What else could she say? Samantha stepped back automatically. 'Um—is something wrong?'

It was a foolish question. Something was obviously wrong, or Matthew's mother wouldn't be here. Images of herself and Matthew in various stages of undress flashed guiltily before Samantha's eyes. Dear God, she hadn't seen them, had she? Samantha fretted. The door hadn't been locked then. Matthew had remarked upon it.

The older woman said nothing until Samantha had closed the door behind her. Then, linking her hands together at her waist, she paused in the middle of the floor.

'I'm afraid I've got some bad news,' she said, and for an awful moment Samantha was afraid that something dreadful had happened to Matthew. She clasped her hands, and pressed them to her throat, feeling absurdly as if she was choking. But his mother's next words removed that fear, and replaced it with another. 'I have to tell you, on his behalf, that Matthew's had to return to London.'

'To London!'

Samantha blinked, and Caroline Putnam nodded. 'Yes. I'm afraid there's been something of an emergency. Melissa—that is, the girl we all hope Matthew will eventually marry—has been involved in—in an accident. Naturally, as soon as he heard, he made arrangements to fly back to England to be with her.'

A mixture of feelings swept over Samantha at that moment. Dismay; disbelief; indignation. How could Matthew have gone back to London and left her here, whatever the emergency? He must know how she would feel. How could he do this to her?

'I'm sure this must have come as a shock to you,' Caroline was saying now, and Samantha knew she had to hide her real feelings. There was no way she was going to let Matthew—or his mother—know how humiliated they had made her feel. She had to pretend her reaction was one of inconvenience.

'Oh, dear,' she said, turning aside so that she could surreptitiously dry her damp palms on her skirt. 'What a nuisance!'

'Yes.' But Matthew's mother was not as gullible as all that. 'He's hurt you, hasn't he? I was afraid he would.'

'No!' Samantha's response was more defensive than she would have liked, but the other woman's words had stung. She didn't want anybody feeling sorry for her. 'I—our relationship was never serious, Mrs Putnam. If Matthew told you that it was, then he was exaggerating.'

'Well—no. No, he didn't.' Samantha winced. She had never expected he had. 'But I know, from personal experience, you understand, that my son can be totally insensitive.'

There wasn't a lot Samantha could say to that. 'I agree' sprang most readily to mind, but that would have sounded too much like the resentment she was desperate to hide.

'Anyway, I—just wanted to warn you,' Caroline continued after a moment. 'And—naturally you're welcome to stay for the rest of the weekend, if that's what you'd like to do.'

That was her cue, Samantha realised bitterly. No one, least of all Matthew's mother, really wanted her to stay for the rest of the weekend. This wasn't just a social gathering; it was a family party. And now that Matthew had gone, she had no legitimate reason to remain.

'Um—that's very kind of you,' she said now, watching the wary expression on the older woman's face. Was Caroline really afraid she might call her bluff, and accept her invitation? For a malicious moment Samantha was tempted to hesitate, just to get her own back. But she didn't. 'However, I think I'd rather go, if you don't mind.'

Caroline's relief was almost palpable. 'Of course I don't mind,' she said. 'But I'm afraid you won't be able to leave until tomorrow morning. I'll arrange for Niarchos to come and pick you up. Would nine-thirty be all right? Or perhaps a little later?'

'Nine-thirty would be fine,' replied Samantha firmly, and Caroline smiled.

'Good. I'll have my secretary check out the times of flights to England. I'm sure that won't be a problem. There are several flights in and out of Athens every day.'

'Fine.'

Samantha adopted what she hoped was an equally determined smile, and waited for Caroline to leave. She had done what she came for with obvious success. So why was she waiting? What more did she have to say?

'Er—about supper——'

Samantha stiffened. 'Yes?'

'I—we'll—quite understand if you'd rather have it here, in your room,' Matthew's mother ventured smoothly, and, although until that moment that was exactly what Samantha had wished, the older woman's insensitivity struck a nerve.

'Oh, I don't think so,' she responded now, realising exactly what Matthew's family would think if she didn't appear. Poor cow, they'd titter, only it would sound somewhat different in their language. Too embarrassed to show her face, now that Matthew's deserted her! 'I'd like to join you, if you have no objections. It's such a lovely evening. It seems a shame to waste it.'

Which was why Samantha found herself sitting on the terrace wall some time later, gazing somewhat tearfully at the moon. It was all very well pretending a brashness she didn't feel, but she wasn't as thick-skinned as Caroline imagined. It had taken an enormous amount of courage to walk into a crowded room earlier that evening and behave as if she had a right to be there. Oh, she had been introduced to many of the other guests that afternoon, and one of them, at least—Matthew's cousin, Alex—had made no secret of his willingness to take Matthew's place. But, without the man who had brought her here, she felt very much the outsider, and that was why, after the meal, she'd escaped outdoors.

She wondered what Matthew was doing at this moment. She wondered what emergency had necessitated his presence. Had Prince Georgio had an accident, perhaps? Or had Melissa simply broken her engagement?

Whichever it was, and whatever Matthew had said, his family still expected him to be the one to marry her. So what was he doing with her? Samantha sniffed. Was it all a game to him, or was he trying to make Melissa jealous?

She shook her head, and tried to take pleasure in her surroundings. It was a beautiful evening. By moonlight the water looked dark and mysterious, and the sky was a silver-studded arc of blackness overhead. From indoors, the plaintive sound of bouzouki music stirred her senses. There was a breeze, too; quite a cool breeze, that brought the scent of Havana tobacco drifting to her nostrils. It should have been a night for love, but instead Matthew was far away in London, comforting a woman who was engaged to someone else . . .

'You do not find the view to your liking, Miss Maxwell?'

The gruff, accented voice came out of the darkness, somewhere to her right, and Samantha started violently. She had been unaware that she was not alone on the terrace. She had believed everyone was inside, indulging in the impromptu dances Greek music always seemed to inspire. They were rehearsing for tomorrow evening, when a group of musicians had been hired for the occasion. Samantha had heard all about it from Henry Purham before Caroline's scrutiny—and her own despair—had driven her to seek this quiet sanctuary.

Now, she turned her head and saw the glowing tip of a cigar. And, as her eyes adjusted to the shadows, she saw it was Matthew's grandfather, sitting watching her, framed by a fan-backed cane chair.

She had met him earlier. Caroline had performed the introduction—if introduction was the right word for the perfunctory presentation she had made. It had been a reluctant duty at best, and she had made sure Samantha was not allowed to stay around and make any embarrassing comments. Matthew's mother had taken her off on the pretext of wanting to introduce her to someone else, and so far as Samantha was aware he had forgotten her. But apparently not.

'I'm sorry,' she said now, sliding down off the wall, and showing every indication of leaving. 'I didn't realise I was intruding.'

'You are not.' The old man frowned. 'Please.' He pointed to another chair, set at right angles to his own. 'Join me.'

Samantha hesitated. 'It's very kind of you, but—really—I was just going in.'

'Were you?' He sounded disconcertingly like Matthew. 'You looked quite at home before I spoke to you. A little sad, perhaps, but in no particular hurry to seek the isolation of your apartments.'

Samantha allowed a breath to escape her. 'I—don't think we have anything to say to one another, Mr Apollonius,' she said quietly. 'And—I have packing to do. I'm leaving in the morning.'

'Yes. So Caroline tells me.' He paused. 'This is your decision?'

'Yes.' Samantha nodded.

'Does my grandson know?'

Samantha suppressed the retort that sprang to her lips. 'Perhaps,' she said, smoothing her hands over her skirt. 'It doesn't really matter. He's not here any more, and I should never have come.'

'So why did you?'

Matthew's grandfather raised his cigar to his lips, and regarded her intently. It was not an unexpected question, and yet Samantha was unprepared for it. It was reasonable enough that he should want to know. But she had the feeling he already knew the answer.

'Because—because Matt—Matthew—invited me,' she replied, glancing over her shoulder, towards the lights of the villa. 'I'm sorry if you think it was an imposition. But—I didn't know anything about—about your grandson, until I saw this place.'

The old man's eyes narrowed, but whether it was with scepticism, or simply the effects of the cigar smoke, Samantha couldn't be sure. 'What do you mean?' he asked. 'What did you not know?'

'Oh, really——' Samantha didn't want to get into this, particularly as she was fairly sure he wouldn't believe her. 'I made a mistake, that's all,' she offered, shrugging. 'And, contrary to your suggestion, I love the view.'

Aristotle's mouth compressed. 'You did not know Matthew was my grandson?' he persisted, and Samantha sighed.

'No.'

'You knew his name?'

'Putnam. Yes, I knew his name.'

'And the company he owns?'

'I didn't know he owned it, but yes. I knew about J.P. Software!'

The old man studied her taut face. 'That was said with some feeling. Do I take it you have had some dealings with J.P. Software? Is that how you met my grandson?'

'No.' Samantha shook her head. 'No.'

'Then tell me.' The old man gestured to the chair again. 'And sit down.'

Samantha's fists clenched, but, short of defying him, there was little she could do. So, with obvious misgivings, she came and took the chair beside him, moving it a few inches away from his, before subsiding on to the cushioned seat.

'Good.' Aristotle regarded her submission with evident satisfaction. 'Now I do not have to keep tilting my head to look at you. And, at my age, it is very pleasant to have the company of a beautiful woman.'

Samantha's features felt stiff. He didn't have to do this, she thought. He didn't have to say these things to get her to tell him how Matthew brought her here. It wasn't a secret, after all. Caroline probably knew all about it.

'So,' he prompted. 'Tell me how you met my grandson.'

Samantha bent her head. 'It's a long story.'

'We have all night.'

Samantha gave him a half-rueful look. 'I'm sure you know already.'

'No. No, I do not. He told me you ran a small café, that is all. I am curious to hear how he introduced himself.'

That again! Samantha's mouth flattened. What he really wanted to hear was how she could pretend not to know who he was, when his grandfather was so famous. Perhaps he thought Matthew would have told her. If he did, he knew his grandson as little as she did.

'There was a party,' she said slowly. 'I did the catering, and—Matt was there. End of story.'

'Beginning of story,' Aristotle corrected her, puffing on his cigar. 'I assume my grandson asked to see you again.'

'Not then, no.' Samantha took a wary breath. 'Look, I was—*I am*—engaged to someone else. I told Matt I couldn't see him. But—he wouldn't take no for an answer.'

'That sounds like my grandson,' remarked the old man drily. 'And ultimately, it seems, he had his way.'

In more ways than one, thought Samantha, though she didn't voice it. 'You could say that,' she agreed, pleating her skirt with trembling fingers. 'He got—someone else—to offer me a catering assignment at J.P. Software. Then, when I got there, I found out it was him.'

Aristotle frowned. 'Someone else? Who?'

'I don't know.' Samantha lifted her shoulders. 'Someone called—Burgess! If that was his real name.'

'Ah. Victor.'

'You know him?' Samantha couldn't hide her curiosity.

'Yes.' The old man inclined his head. 'Victor Burgess is my grandson's valet, for want of a better word. He refused to have a bodyguard, so Victor was installed.'

'A bodyguard!' Samantha stared at him. 'Why does Matt need a bodyguard?'

'He is my grandson,' said Aristotle simply. 'I regret that there are too many unscrupulous men around who would stop at nothing to get their hands on my family.'

'Kidnapping?' Samantha was appalled,

'Kidnapping; extortion; murder! The list is endless, Miss Maxwell. And Matthew is so independent. That is why he formed his own company. To prove he doesn't need me or my money.'

Samantha caught her breath. 'Oh, I'm sure that isn't true...'

'Are you?' The old man's lips twisted. 'But how well do you know my grandson?' He paused. 'Not very well,

I'm afraid. *Dhen pirazi*, one day he will have to take my place.'

Samantha watched as he crushed the remains of his cigar in a crystal ashtray. For a moment she actually felt sorry for him. In spite of everything, she was sure he loved his grandson. There was a certain wistfulness in his words that betrayed it.

'I'd better go,' she murmured, shifting to the edge of her chair, but his outstretched hand detained her.

'You said you were—betrothed,' he ventured, the old-fashioned word sounding almost musical on his lips. 'So, why did you come away with Matthew?'

'Because I was a fool,' replied Samantha, shaking off his hand and getting to her feet. 'Don't worry, Mr Apollonius. I shan't be seeing your grandson again.'

CHAPTER TEN

'WHERE is she?'

Matthew strode angrily across his mother's bedroom and came to loom over her, his hands gripping the vanity unit on either side of her shrinking figure. She could feel the aggression pulsing from him, and his reflected image in the mirror in front of her was dark and threatening. She found it hard to keep his face in focus, and for the first time in her life Caroline felt intimidated.

'Where do you think?' she exclaimed now, making a brave effort to continue with her make-up. But the hand holding the mascara brush slipped, and a streak of charcoal smeared her cheek. 'Damn!' she muttered. 'Matthew, will you get away from me?'

'When you tell me what you said to her,' retorted her son grimly, as she dabbed ineffectually at the mascara with a tissue. 'You knew I was coming back. I said I'd be here for Apollo's party, and I am. So what the hell did you say to send her back to England? I told you to explain.' He straightened. 'God! I should have known better than to trust you! I should have spoken to her myself.'

Caroline quivered as he moved away from her. 'I understood you'd tried to speak to her yourself,' she retorted, flinching when his savage gaze impaled her once again. 'Well—you said she wouldn't open the door,' she protested.

'I said the door was locked,' Matthew declared inflexibly. 'I did not say she wouldn't open it. She must have been in the bathroom or something, and couldn't hear me.' His eyes darkened. 'And you were so eager for me to go.'

'I was worried about Melissa,' replied his mother defensively. 'And you must have been, too, or you wouldn't have gone rushing off like that.'

'Yes—well, we both know what a fiasco that was, don't we?' he stated scornfully. 'Just tell me, did you have anything to do with it, by any chance?'

'Matthew!'

She gazed at him indignantly, but Matthew gazed back without remorse. 'It's not beyond your capabilities,' he retorted, pushing his hands back into the pockets of his dark trousers, and pacing nerve-rackingly about the room. 'You're the one who's always agitating for me to get married and settle down. Did you really think Melissa's pathetic attempt to get attention would succeed, when all her other efforts didn't?'

His mother winced. 'That's a cruel and heartless thing to say, Matthew!'

'But true, nevertheless,' he essayed coldly. 'Half a dozen paracetamol tablets hardly warrants the time and trouble the doctors and nurses took over her. And let's get it in perspective, shall we? Ivanov had found out she'd been sleeping with someone else. Not me,' he added hastily, before Caroline could even consider it. 'Melissa's a hot little body. She always was. And apparently Ivanov doesn't keep her—happy—in that area.' His lips twisted. 'Her words were rather less polite, but suffice it to say she thinks certain parts of his anatomy are as frozen as the steppes he comes from.'

'I don't wish to hear that.' Caroline reached for a jar of moisturiser, and unscrewed the cap with slightly unsteady fingers. 'I can't believe Melissa could be so foolish!'

'No.' Matthew conceded the point without rancour. 'But then, we all do foolish things when our emotions are involved.'

His mother's head jerked up. 'You mean you regret not marrying her when you had the chance?'

'No.' Matthew was adamant, and his expression had darkened again. 'I mean *you* did a foolish thing when you sent Sam back to England. Did you really think it would make any difference? Out of sight, out of mind—is that what you thought?'

Caroline's nostrils flared. 'You mean you intend seeing that young woman again?'

'Yes.' Matthew paused behind her again, and his eyes were disturbingly intent. 'And don't call her "that young woman". Her name's Sam—Samantha. I suggest you get used to it.'

His mother's cheeks gained a little colour, but this time she didn't back down. 'Well, I can't stop you, of course,' she said tersely, smoothing cream over the offending smear of mascara. 'But you might be interested to hear I didn't *send* Miss Maxwell back to England. She left of her own accord. It was all her idea.'

'I don't believe you.'

Her son's response was almost instantaneous, but for the first time since he had stormed into her room Caroline sensed a faint hesitation. Dear God, she thought, her hands stilling automatically as the amazing idea occurred to her. Matthew wasn't sure of her. He actually had some doubts.

She blinked, and wiped her fingers on a cotton-wool ball. Of all the scenarios she had entertained during the past twenty-four hours, the idea that that ordinary young woman might not be besotted with her son had never even occurred to her. Oh, it was true she had offered to leave without much prompting. But Caroline knew she had been instrumental in promoting that decision. She hadn't given her a whole lot of choice. But she wondered now if she could have been mistaken. What if the girl hadn't been as upset as she'd thought? She had made a show of not caring, but Caroline had discounted that. She had assumed it was just an act, put on to protect her sensibilities. But what if it hadn't been? What if her son was besotted by that girl?

It didn't bear thinking about. He was just on the rebound, she told herself. Matthew was still infatuated with Melissa.

But if that was so, and Melissa's engagement to Prince Georgio had foundered, why was he here? Melissa still wanted him; that was obvious. It was why she had asked for him as she was being whisked away to the hospital to have her stomach pumped, or something equally ghastly. And it had seemed such an opportune coincidence: that Matthew should have been with that girl, when Melissa's attempted suicide was reported. Caroline couldn't have asked for anything more guaranteed to cause a rift between them. And, just when everything seemed to be going right, it was turning out all wrong.

She sighed. She might not always have approved of Melissa—and she had certainly resented the disastrous effect the break-up of their relationship had had on her son—but Melissa was good-looking, and personable, and she would make Matthew a tolerable wife. If only her son had ever wanted to get married. But he hadn't.

She supposed she couldn't entirely blame him. Her own ambivalent attitude towards the married state, and his uncle's vicissitudes aside, Matthew was not exactly surrounded by examples of nuptial bliss. His best friend had been married and divorced twice, and his Greek relations tended to use marriage to perpetuate a dynasty. Even her father had not been above taking a mistress when, after Caroline was born, her own mother had proved so disappointingly unproductive. Her son had grown up seeing a succession of other women pass through his grandfather's house, and she could hardly complain if he rebelled against their hypocrisy. Besides, he knew that getting married would mean an end to his individual lifestyle. If he had a wife, he wouldn't be able to deny his identity any longer.

Caroline passed a rather bemused hand across her cheek. It couldn't be true. She was over-reacting. Just because Matthew had shown her a side of his personality she had hitherto not encountered, she was anticipating problems that didn't exist. He was annoyed because she had upset his plans for the weekend, that was all. Well, for heaven's sake, he could do without a woman for one night!

'I said I don't believe you,' he grated now, and she became aware that he was still standing, glowering at her in the mirror. She hoped he couldn't read her mind. The thoughts she had been having were not for publication.

'Well, it's true,' she replied, after a moment, not finding it particularly easy to pick up the threads of their conversation. 'She insisted on leaving first thing this morning.' She crossed her fingers, and then continued firmly, 'I think she'd have left last night, if I hadn't persuaded her otherwise.'

Matthew's mouth compressed. 'Shit!' he muttered succinctly, and in spite of her aversion to his language Caroline's most immediate reaction was one of alarm.

'Really, Matt!' she exclaimed, in a desperate attempt to salvage something from this situation. She adopted a determinedly amused tone. 'You'd think you were in love with the girl!'

Samantha's father came to the café on Monday lunchtime. It wasn't unusual to see him there, but it was unusual for him to leave his table vacant. Instead of sitting down, Mr Maxwell smiled at Debbie, and then walked around behind the display cases to where his daughter was busy preparing sandwiches.

'Sam,' he said, distracting her attention from the chutney she was spooning from a jar. 'Can I have a word?'

'Dad!' Samantha didn't know whether to be anxious or relieved. It was so unexpected of him to make the café a place for them to talk in, and although she thought she could guess what he wanted she wished she'd had more notice of his intention.

'Can we talk?' he repeated, and Samantha glanced around at Debbie, who was hovering by the till.

'I—suppose so,' she said, the look she cast her assistant indicative of her feelings. 'We'll go into the office,' she added, wiping her hands on a tissue. 'Take over, will you, Deb? I'll be as quick as I can.'

Debbie nodded, clearly intrigued by Mr Maxwell's visit, and Samantha led the way into the tiny office, not without some misgivings. It was obvious Debbie would want to know what was going on. Mr Maxwell had never interfered with the running of the café before. She was bound to think it was something serious.

'Your mother asked me to talk to you,' declared Samantha's father, without preamble, as soon as the door was wedged closed behind them. 'She's worried sick over this business with Paul. You can't seriously intend breaking your engagement. Why, you and he have been inseparable since you were in your teens.'

Samantha sighed. 'The engagement's broken, Dad. I spoke to Paul last night. And as for us being inseparable: perhaps that's what was wrong with our relationship. We've been so close to each other, we've never had the chance to see anyone else.'

Mr Maxwell breathed out heavily. 'Sam——' He spread his hands in a helpless gesture. 'Sam, you can't do this. Not just on a whim.'

'It's not a whim, Dad. I mean what I say. It's not fair to Paul to carry on. I don't love him. I don't think I ever did. Not in the proper way, anyway.'

'The proper way!' her father mimicked impatiently. 'What is the "proper" way? I doubt if you know. I know I don't. It's mixing with these well-to-do people, isn't it? They've unsettled you. Given you ideas about making money and getting rich quick!'

'That's not true!' Samantha was indignant. 'I've got no plans, beyond continuing to run the café as I've always done. I've told you I'm not going to accept any more commissions. What more can I say?'

Mr Maxwell grimaced. 'Then what's wrong with Paul all of a sudden? You told your mother there was no one else. Is that true?'

Samantha caught her breath. 'Yes. Yes, it's true,' she declared forcefully. 'I just don't want to get married. Is there anything wrong with that?'

'Yes, there is.' Her father regarded her frustratedly. 'You know your mother's been looking forward to organising the wedding. Why, she's even made a provisional guest list, and talked about what she and I could get you. We thought a couple of thousand pounds towards your mortgage wouldn't come amiss. And what with Paul being an estate agent and all, he's bound to have an insight into what kind of property you should buy.'

Samantha drew a breath. 'No, Dad.'

'What do you mean, no? Of course, he will——'

'I mean, no. I'm not going to marry Paul,' said Samantha flatly. 'I'm sorry if you're disappointed, and I'm sorry if Mum was looking forward to being the mother of the bride, but this time I've got to do what *I* think is best. Not you.'

'This time?' Mr Maxwell frowned. 'Are you saying we've interfered in your life before?'

'Oh, Dad!' Samantha groaned. 'I know that anything you've done for me has been with my best interests at heart. But, believe me, marrying Paul would be a mistake. I know that now. So can't you be thankful I found out, before I had to face a messy divorce?'

Her father stared at her. 'You said you know that *now*. Why now? Something must have happened to make you change your mind.'

Samantha wanted to scream, but she didn't. Instead, she pushed her hands into her apron pockets, and faced her father bravely. 'All right,' she said, hearing the catch in her voice, and doing her best to disguise it. 'I had an affair.' She let that news sink in, and then she added briskly, 'But it's over now. I shan't be seeing him again.'

'But you told your mother——'

'I lied.' Samantha held up her hand. 'Or, at least, I didn't tell her the whole truth. There is no one else.' She paused, and then added uncomfortably, 'There was—but there isn't now.'

Her father looked stunned. 'An affair!' he echoed weakly. 'Oh, Sam!'

'It's not the end of the world!' exclaimed Samantha tersely, her own nerves dangerously near to breaking-point. 'As I say, it's over now, and no harm done.' At least, she hoped not. Matthew had probably assumed she was on the Pill. Until he discovered she hadn't been with a man, of course. But, by then, it was too late.

'But an affair,' protested her father helplessly, and Samantha realised how naïve he was in this day and age. It was partly her fault, she supposed. Her relationship with Paul had shielded her from the common demands of her generation, and they had all become a little smug because of it. But life wasn't like that, and she should have realised her bland existence could only survive in limbo.

'I'm sorry, Dad,' she apologised now, feeling a little guilty for springing it on him this way. 'I didn't want to hurt you.'

'No.' Mr Maxwell shook his head. 'No, I suppose you didn't.' He paused. 'Have you told Paul?'

'Not yet.' Samantha shrugged. 'He—still thinks he can get me to change my mind. I don't think he'll be so eager when I tell him what I've done.'

'Oh, Sam!' Her father sighed. 'You've shocked me, you really have. I never would have thought it of you.'

'No.' Samantha conceded the point. 'If it's any consolation, nor would I.'

Which didn't augur well for the rest of the day. Mr
Maxwell left without even having his usual sandwich, and
Samantha spent the remainder of the lunch period in a
state of weary aggravation. She felt like a child again,
who'd just received a dressing-down from the school
head. She was twenty-four years old, and had been running her own business for over two years, and she still felt
as crushed as a teenager. For heaven's sake, she argued
silently, what she'd done was no big deal. Not really.
Most of her friends had had affairs before they'd left
college.

But they weren't engaged, she admitted ruefully, and
if she'd been so desperate to spread her wings, why
couldn't she have done it with someone else, someone she
could at least respect? Matthew Putnam was the pits. He
was a cheat and a liar, and he hadn't a grain of decency
in his body. He had thought nothing about seducing her
and then rushing off to see Melissa. She hoped the other
woman gave him hell. He deserved it for what he'd done
to her.

Or did he? Samantha sighed. The truth was, she didn't
like herself any better. What bugged her most was the fact
that, if Matthew hadn't walked out as he had, she'd most
probably have agreed to continue the affair until he got
tired of her. It was so humiliating. She'd been so sure he
still wanted her, particularly after those unforgettable
hours in her bed. When his mother had told her he had
left to go back to London to be with Melissa, she had
been completely devastated. It had even crossed her mind
that Mrs Putnam might be making the whole thing up,
and that was why she had deliberately joined the rest of

the family for supper. But it had been true. The looks—sometimes sympathetic, sometimes malicious—that had been cast in her direction as she ate had convinced her of that. And Matthew's grandfather had only confirmed her suspicions. She didn't know Matthew at all.

At least it had brought her to her senses, she reflected later that afternoon, after Debbie had gone to get her bus. Given the fact that Matthew was not to be relied on, wasn't it better to realise it now, rather than spend weeks—months even—pursuing a goal that didn't exist? He had hurt her, it was true, but she'd get over it. And she hadn't had time to feel his loss.

She was about to leave the café to go home when someone rattled the door. 'We're closed,' she called, collecting her bag and keys from the office, and threading her way between the tables. She adjusted the blind and opened the door. 'I'm sorry, we——'

Her voice trailed away into silence. Mondays were usually busy days, and it wasn't unusual for customers to try and get served after hours. She had assumed it was one of the small-holders from the market, wanting a cup of tea and a toasted teacake before driving home. But it wasn't. It was Matthew. And, for all her much-vaunted practicality, her knees wobbled.

'Can I come in?' he asked, his eyes rooting disturbingly on her mouth, and Samantha let out her breath in a rush. He was the last person she had expected to see, and it took longer than she had expected to pull her wits together.

'I—no,' she denied, after a moment, though his leather-clad frame successfully blocked her exit. 'I was just leaving,' she added, as if it was relevant. 'Please will you get out of my way?'

Matthew didn't move, except to raise one arm and rest it against the wooden frame. From that position of dominance, he looked down at her half impatiently, and she wished she hadn't opened the door and given him the advantage.

'I have to talk to you, Sam,' he said, and, although she was sure this was all just another move in the game to him, there was no trace of humour in his eyes. On the contrary, they were red-rimmed, and brooding, and painfully intent. They roamed over her face and figure with a thoroughness she would have found insolent from anyone else. But she was in such a nervous state that she didn't have time to object to his appraisal.

'I don't think we have anything to talk about,' she said tersely, desperate for some way to get him off her door-step. 'Look, we've had this conversation before, and nothing's changed. You and I—we just don't have anything in common. I was a fool to let you talk me into going to Delphus, and now I'd like to forget all about it.'

'That's not true, and you know it.' Matthew's voice was harsh. He glanced up and down the High Street, as if gauging whether their altercation was attracting any attention. Then, without giving her notice of his intentions, he removed his arm from the door frame and used it to propel her back into the empty café. And, with his shoulders against the glass panels, the door closed heavily behind him. 'Now,' he said, unzipping his jerkin to reveal an open-necked shirt of dark green silk, 'let's drop the "I don't know what you're doing here" routine, shall we? We have some unfinished business. I want to know why you walked out on me.'

'Why *I* walked out on *you*!' Samantha caught her breath, but his audacity gave her the spurt she needed.

'Forgive me, but I was under the impression that you had walked out on me! How is Miss Mainwaring, by the way? All the better for seeing you, no doubt.'

Matthew's lips tightened. 'All right. I deserved that, I suppose. I did leave without seeing you, but my mother explained, didn't she? Melissa's mother was fairly frantic on the phone, and I guess she believed it was more serious than it was. Sufficiently so that I didn't ask questions. I just grabbed a ride with Spiro, and took the next plane back to London.'

Samantha managed not to show any emotion at this evidence of his continuing involvement with Melissa. Indeed, with every word he spoke she was growing colder and colder. His arrogance appalled her. What kind of a woman did he think she was?

'It doesn't matter,' she said now, still finding it difficult to meet his gaze without flinching. She checked the clasp of her handbag, and tucked it under her arm with businesslike firmness. Anything to avoid looking at the brown column of his throat emerging from the open neck of his shirt. Or remembering how smooth his skin had felt beneath her hands, with its light but silky pelt of fine dark hair.

'Don't say that.' Matthew made a sound that was suspiciously like a moan, and straightened away from the door. 'Sam, you have to believe me when I tell you, I'd never have gone if I'd known then what I know now. They said she'd tried to commit suicide. They said she'd been rushed to the hospital, and that she was presently undergoing treatment. What was I supposed to think? My God, they made it sound as if it was all my fault!'

'And was it?' Samantha's question was automatic.

'No.' Matthew raked restless fingers through his hair. 'Sam—Melissa and I—that's history. I don't care if I never see her again.'

That brought her head up, but the heat radiating from Matthew's eyes made her look away again. It also brought a little bloom of colour blossoming in her neck, and she put a nervous hand to her throat.

'I—I'm not really interested,' she declared at last, concentrating on the fact that there was a menu missing from the table in the window. 'How you choose to treat your ex-girlfriends is entirely up to you. I've told you how I feel. I wish you'd go away, and let me get on with my life.'

'Like hell!' With the oath still issuing from his tongue, he closed the space between them, his hands descending on her shoulders with unmistakable intent. 'You want me,' he muttered unsteadily, forcing her chin up with his thumbs, so that he could see her face. 'No. Don't look away from me. We want each other, Sam. You know it as well as I do. God, baby, did you honestly think I'd let you go?'

Samantha shivered. It was the moment of truth, and she was no more ready for it now than she had ever been. The grip of his hands, the heat of his skin, the heady scent of the soap he used, which mingled with the sharper odour of his body, all combined to seduce her reason. She had never dreamed he might come after her; never imagined that, having sent her back to London, he might want to see her again. The memory of his lovemaking came back to torment her, and an actual physical ache for the pleasure he had taught her was sapping her resistance.

But it was only lust, she warned herself repeatedly. He wanted her; the undisguised arousal of his body showed her that. But that was all. As she had assured herself many times on the flight back from Athens, he had never pretended otherwise. Apart from anything else, she didn't fit into his world. With Matthew, there could be no lasting commitment.

So, though it took every ounce of will-power she possessed, Samantha forced herself to remain passive in his arms. She didn't attempt to fight him. She knew from past experience that that would do no good. When it came to brute strength, Matthew would always have the upper hand. And she had no desire to cause a conflagration that might consume them both.

'Damn you!' Matthew cupped her face in his strong hands and gazed down at her with dark frustrated eyes. 'Damn you,' he muttered again. 'Don't do this to me, Sam. You know how I feel about you. I would have come sooner, only I'd promised the old man I'd stay for his birthday party. I haven't slept a wink since I left Delphus on Friday night.'

Samantha steeled herself. Matthew in any mood was attractive. Matthew in this mood was well-nigh irresistible.

'I—can't help that,' she got out jerkily. 'You—you should have stayed with Melissa. I'm sure she'd have been only too happy——'

'Will you shut the hell up about Melissa?' he snarled menacingly. 'I don't give a damn about Melissa!'

'That's not what your mother said.'

The words were unwise, and impulsive. She knew that as soon as they were uttered, but it was too late then. His brows descended, and his thumbs dug almost painfully into her cheekbones. 'My mother?' he echoed. 'What—exactly—did my mother tell you?'

Samantha's shoulders made an involuntary gesture. 'She—she just said that you—that she—hoped—you'd eventually marry Melissa——'

'My God!'

'—and that—that—was what the rest of the family hoped as well.'

'*Beautiful*!' On Matthew's lips it was an oath. 'And you believed her?'

Samantha shrugged. 'I've told you, I—it's nothing to do with me.' She paused, and then went on doggedly, 'I've had time to think, and I realise now that it was probably the best thing that could happen. We're from two different worlds, Matt. It was never going to work, and you know it.'

'You don't mean that.'

'I do.' Samantha gathered strength from the look of uncertainty on his face. 'There was never going to be any future for our relationship. I was just a novelty. I belonged to someone else, and you couldn't bear to think I might prefer Paul to you.'

Matthew's mouth flattened. 'You didn't sleep with Paul.'

'No.' Samantha held up her head. 'Because he had too much respect for me as a person——'

'Respect be damned,' retorted Matthew harshly. 'You didn't sleep with him because he didn't make you feel the way I do. Don't trivialise what we had together. It was good——'

'It wasn't real,' she protested, but his continued nearness was wearing her down.

'That's not true.' Matthew's hands left her face to shape her throat, and then moved down, over the quivering sides of her breasts, to the slender swell of her hips.

He watched her as his hands explored her body, and it was the hardest thing Samantha had ever done to stand still in his grasp. 'It was so real, it was the best thing that ever happened to me,' he told her huskily. 'I want you in my life, Sam. You're warm, and passionate, and endlessly desirable. I want you to come and live with me. I've only got an apartment at the moment, but if you'd rather we lived in a house then we'll buy one. All things are possible, because I love you. If you care for me at all, for God's sake don't turn me down.'

Samantha trembled. She couldn't believe it. Matthew had said he loved her. He had actually said he loved her. Dear God, what was she supposed to do now?

And, as if the bemused expression that had crossed her face at his words had given him some encouragement, he bent his head and caressed her ear with his tongue. 'Don't look so surprised,' he whispered with wry humour, his hands on her hips urging her against his heavy arousal. 'You don't imagine I enjoy living in a constant state of frustration, do you?'

Samantha couldn't speak. Her cheek was pressed against the soft leather of his jerkin and the skin of his throat was only inches from her lips. She could see the shadow of his chest hair under his silk shirt, and knew it arrowed down to the virile pubescence that cradled his manhood. She already knew how that felt against her softness. In fact, it was frightening to realise how familiar she was with his lean body, and how vivid were the memories his words conjured up.

'I—can't,' she got out at last, fighting for her own salvation, and Matthew let out a strangled cry.

'Why can't you?' he demanded, drawing back to rest his forehead against hers. 'You want me. I know you do.

And—you may even learn to love me one day. So long as we're together, I'm prepared to take the chance.'

'Well, I'm not.' In spite of the fact that his mouth was only inches from her own, and the temptation to taste it was almost unbearable, she had to keep her head. 'Is—is this what you told Melissa?' she asked, her hands firm against his jacket. 'Before she realised you had no intention of marrying her?'

'Oh, God!' Matthew groaned. 'I thought I told you to forget about Melissa. My relationship with her was never like this, believe me. I may have thought I loved her once, but now I know differently.' He gave a grim laugh. 'Do I ever!'

Samantha swallowed. 'So what are you saying?' She was sure she already knew the answer, but she had to know. 'Is this—a proposal?'

'A proposal!'

In the seconds before Matthew could avert his gaze, she saw the stunned expression in his eyes, and her heart faltered. She had known it all along, of course. Nothing could have been further from the truth. Matthew didn't want a wife—particularly not someone like her. He wanted something entirely different.

But, even as she wrenched herself away from him, he was recovering his confidence. 'Sam,' he began, the beguiling softness of his voice belying the insensitivity of his words, 'don't you think one engagement is enough for the time being?'

'You——'

Words escaped her, and before she could summon up the right ones to get him out of there the door behind them opened, and Paul Webster stepped into the café.

'Sam,' he said, eyebrows raised, his voice cool and suspicious. He looked at Matthew, then back at Samantha. 'Is something wrong?'

Samantha felt an insane desire to laugh. Of all the people to walk into the café, it had to be Paul. Of course, she'd known the night before, when she gave him back his ring, that he hadn't believed she really meant it. But, even so, she hadn't expected him to turn up here today. It was just as if last night had never happened, and she didn't know whether to be glad or sorry.

Matthew's eyes had narrowed as he surveyed the other man's appearance, and Samantha guessed he wasn't pleased. The fact that she hadn't had time to tell him yet that she had broken her engagement now seemed like rough justice. Was he wondering how she was going to handle it? Was he worried that she might tell Paul that he had seduced her?

But no. With bitter logic she knew that Matthew was unlikely to worry about anything. And she was fooling herself if she believed either of them would risk life and limb for her honour. Matthew had no honour, and Paul had no excuse.

'No,' she said at last, realising it was up to her to make whatever amends she could of this situation. There was no point in inflaming tempers with emotive words. For Paul's sake—and for her own self-respect—she had to get rid of Matthew. 'Mr—er—Putnam was just leaving.' Her hostile gaze dared him to deny it. She walked past Paul and opened the door. 'Thank you for your offer,' she added coldly. 'But I don't accept that kind of assignment.'

CHAPTER ELEVEN

MATTHEW strode into his office in the Purcell building, only to halt abruptly at the sight of the man reclining in the chair behind his desk. 'Papa!' he exclaimed, hiding his irritation behind a mask of politeness. He advanced more slowly into the room. 'I didn't know you were in London.'

'No, I know.' For once his grandfather spoke in English. 'I asked your mother not to tell you I was coming.'

'Really?' Matthew's dark brows arched interrogatively. 'Any reason why?'

'Yes. I wanted to be sure you would not invent some non-existent reason for being out of the country when I arrived,' replied Aristotle mildly. His dark eyes, so like his grandson's, glittered with malicious satisfaction. 'I also wanted to see for myself that your mother was not exaggerating.'

Matthew's features stiffened. 'My mother?'

'You did not think she would not share her worries about you with me?' enquired the old man, with rather more animation. '*Thee mou*, Matthew, it is six months since my birthday! Six months since you told me you never wanted to see the Mainwaring woman again!'

'So?' Matthew shrugged.

'So, why does Caroline tell me you are never out of the office these days?' He glanced at the thick gold watch on his wrist. 'Are you aware it is already after nine o'clock in the evening? What are you trying to do, *aghori mou*? Work yourself to death?'

Matthew's mouth flattened. 'Don't be ridiculous!'

'What is ridiculous?' The old man jerked forward angrily. 'Have you looked in a mirror lately? You look— *ill*!'

'No, I don't.' Matthew heaved a sigh, and flung himself into the chair across the desk from his grandfather. 'I'm tired, that's all.'

'Tired!'

'It's true.' Matthew crossed one ankle across his knee, and rested his hand on his thigh. 'I can tell you what I've been doing, if you like. Only you generally say you have no interest in J.P. Software.'

'I don't.'

'There you are, then.' Matthew lifted his shoulders. 'You won't want to hear how I've been rewriting a program for translating English into a foreign language and vice versa. And not just any language, I might add. I've been experimenting with——'

'*Arketa*!' The old man silenced him with an angry gesture. 'You are right. I do not wish to hear how successful you have been in thwarting my efforts to ensure the corporation's future. I am sure that if you had your way you would have me sell off its assets, and put thousands of people out of work. But I cannot do that, and it angers me that you care so little for my feelings.'

'That's not true.' The words were mumbled, but they were audible just the same. 'Of course I care about your feelings, Papa. And, whatever you think, I do know my responsibilities. But—I'm not a boy. I can take care of myself.'

'Can you?' His grandfather didn't sound any more convinced, but there was concern, not irritation, in his voice now. 'Matthew, your mother is worried about you. And frankly, having seen you for myself, so am I. She says you do not eat enough, and you have obviously lost weight. Must I take it that you are drinking again?' He gestured towards his grandson's appearance. '*Thee mou*, this is not just the result of overwork!'

Matthew tipped his head back on his shoulders. 'Leave it, Papa. I'm all right, really. And I'm not drinking— well, not to excess anyway. But we all need a little stimulation sometimes. Even you.'

His grandfather shook his head. 'That woman has a lot to answer for,' he snapped bitterly.

'What woman?' Matthew's head tipped forward again, his eyes dark and wary.

'Why—the Mainwaring woman, naturally,' complained his grandfather irritably. 'What I do not understand is, why do you not marry her and have done with it? You know that was why she got engaged to Ivanov. And you told me yourself she was never in any danger of taking her own life. It was just her way of trying to get you back. And she is still in London. Caroline tells me so. Why, only the other day your mother met her at some charity function or other. She may be a fool, but she obviously cares about you——'

'Papa!' Matthew's harsh words overrode his grandfather's monologue. 'How many times must I tell you, I don't care that—— ' he snapped his fingers impatiently '—for Melissa's feelings? I know why she put on that act about taking those tablets. I'd made sure she knew about—well, about me taking someone else to Delphus, but she thought she just had to pull my strings and I'd come running. But it didn't work. Oh, I'm not denying I went to see her. How could I do anything else, when I didn't know at that time how serious it might be? But there was never any chance of us resuming our relationship. Believe it, old man, whatever I saw in Melissa is well and truly dead!'

'Then, why——?'

'Why what?' Matthew turned flat, emotionless eyes on him. 'For pity's sake, Papa, don't you and my mother have anything better to do?'

The old man's brows drew together, a bushy grey line above features that were not unlike his grandson's. He stared at Matthew, as if trying to see into his mind, and then uttered a disbelieving snort when his grandson looked away.

'Of course!' he exclaimed, smacking his forehead with the heel of his hand as if punishing himself for not thinking of it sooner. 'I am a fool! I saw it for myself, and I let you persuade me otherwise. It is her, is it not? The other one. The—*kopela* who runs the café!'

'Oh, for God's sake!' Matthew's foot hit the floor with a thud, and he thrust himself up from his chair. 'Why do you do this, Papa? Why can't you accept the fact that it's been a long hard slog, getting this program running? I've worked long hours; I admit it. And I've missed the odd meal here and there; I admit that, too. But I'm not unique. Other people work just as hard. Just because I've lost a little weight, you've let my mother browbeat you into coming here to play the heavy father. Well, it's not necessary. I don't need anyone to hold my hand!'

Aristotle was not intimidated. 'And this is why there are no women in your life?' he enquired mildly. 'Hard work requires celibacy?'

'Maybe.' Matthew fought his way past his indignation, and managed a faint smile. 'Maybe it does,' he repeated, leaving the desk to walk across to the windows. Outside, the lights of the city provided a glittering display, throwing his reflection back at him through the darkened glass. He thrust his hands into his trouser pockets and wished the old man would go. He didn't need anyone else telling him he was losing weight. Loss of weight he could cope with. What he was afraid of was that he was losing his mind.

'So—your association with Miss Maxwell was unproductive?' came his grandfather's voice behind him, and Matthew's hands balled into tight fists.

'It depends what you mean by unproductive,' he responded shortly, as memories of Samantha's soft skin beneath his hands returned to torment him. Desperate to dispel the images that were always more painful after dark, he spoke with rather less caution. 'But if you mean did I make any lasting impression on her life, then perhaps you should ask her husband!'

'Her husband?' Aristotle's slightly stooped figure joined his reflection in the window. 'She was not married when you brought her to Delphus.'

Matthew glanced sideways at him. 'What if she was? Why should you care? As I recall, you've brought a number of married women there yourself.'

'That is beside the point.' The old man sounded tired suddenly. 'The women I knew were older; sophisticated; they knew what they were doing. The Maxwell girl was young, and—I believed—innocent.'

Matthew stared at him. 'How do you know that? You didn't even speak to her.'

'You are wrong.' His grandfather held up his hand. 'That night—the night you went back to England to see Melissa—we talked on the terrace. She was unhappy. I could tell. I suspected it was because your mother had been less than tactful.'

'Hmm.' Matthew remembered the conversation he had had with his mother, after talking to Samantha at the café. Caroline had taken the brunt of his frustration. But even she had had no idea of exactly how desperate he'd felt.

'You did not speak to her yourself, before you left for London?' the old man pressed now, and although since then he hadn't spoken of his feelings to anyone Matthew found himself shaking his head.

'No. She'd locked her door. I couldn't make her hear.'

'And Spiro was waiting to leave, of course.'

Matthew nodded. 'Of course.'

'But you saw her when you got back to England, after that weekend?'

Matthew hesitated. 'Briefly. For about fifteen minutes, to be exact.'

His grandfather frowned, and Matthew guessed he was having to re-think his argument. 'You did not apologise?'

Matthew sighed. 'Of course I apologised!' he exclaimed. And then, because the temptation to confide his real feelings to someone else was just too much, he added wearily, 'I screwed up. I told her how I felt about her, and asked her to come and live with me. She turned me down.'

Aristotle sucked in a breath. 'You asked her to marry you?'

'Not marry, no.' Matthew's tone was flat. 'In any case, she was engaged to someone else.'

'Ah, yes.' His grandfather nodded. 'But the engagement could have been broken, could it not?'

'Maybe.' Matthew heaved a sigh. 'Maybe I didn't want to get married. Maybe I was afraid you'd try and stop us. Maybe I just saw marriage as giving in to what you and my mother expected of me. And, let's face it, my experience of marriage hasn't been good.'

'Because of me,' said his grandfather shrewdly. 'All those women you talked about. I guess you think I should have had more respect for your grandmother.'

'Well, shouldn't you?' suggested Matthew drily, and the old man laughed.

'Perhaps. But your grandmother was not like Miss Maxwell. She did not marry me because she cared about me. Ariadne married me because it was what her father wanted. Because he wished to join his company with mine.' He grimaced. 'That was the start of the Apollonius Corporation, do you know that? Skiathos Ferries and Apollo Shipping! How far we have come since then.'

Matthew shrugged. 'Indeed.'

'So——' His grandfather paused. 'Miss Maxwell is now Mrs——'

'Webster,' supplied Matthew bleakly. 'Her fiancé's name was Paul Webster. I had Victor check him out.'

'Really?' The old man looked reluctantly impressed. 'And the marriage took place—when?'

Matthew turned away. 'June, July. I don't know. Does it matter?'

'It does, if that is what is eating you up inside,' replied his grandfather impatiently. 'Do you mean to tell me you do not even know if they are married? For shame, Matthew! I thought I had taught you better than that.'

Matthew walked to his desk. 'You seem to forget she didn't want me, Papa. That afternoon, when I went to see her, I knew it. As soon as her fiancé turned up, she couldn't wait to get rid of me.'

'Well——' The old man turned to look at him, obviously searching for a reason. 'As you say, they were still engaged.'

Matthew's expression was eloquent of his feelings. 'Nice try, old man, but it won't run. Sam had her chance, but she didn't take it. She'd had her bite of the apple, and she didn't like the taste.'

The wind whistled round a corner of the house, and something blew over on the paved patio her father had had laid the previous year. It was a little unnerving, hearing inanimate objects falling about like live creatures, but the doors and windows were locked, and the storm had been predicted.

Samantha shivered. Perhaps she should have taken her mother's advice and gone with them to Tenerife. Right now, she could have been sitting in a bar, drinking sangria, with nothing more to worry about than what bathing suit she was going to wear to sunbathe in the next day. But the summer flu she had contracted in July had lingered on into September, and she dared not close the café again, and risk losing the rest of her customers.

Not that anyone would really care, she reflected unhappily. Now that she had competition in the High

Street, it was getting harder and harder to hang on to her clientele. And the truth was, her heart wasn't in it any more. Since she had been so ill, she had lost interest in everything.

No, that wasn't precisely true, she corrected herself, reaching for the *TV Times* and scanning the evening's programmes. Actually, she had had no interest in anything since that afternoon Matthew had come to the café. She blinked back the tears that seemed to come so readily to her eyes these days. She should never have sent him away.

It was impossible to read the programme times in her present state, and, tossing the magazine aside, she plucked another chocolate from the open box beside her. An orange cream, she saw dispassionately, biting into its soft centre without really tasting it. She had bought the chocolates that afternoon in the hope that they would cheer her up. But it wasn't much fun eating them alone.

She looked around the cosy sitting-room, and tried to count her blessings. She had a good home, a good family and, aside from a maudlin tendency to feel sorry for herself, she was all right. The café would pick up again once she found another assistant. She shook her head. Imagine Debbie getting married like that! Still, it was probably the best thing for the baby.

Her eyes filled with tears again, and she dashed them away with an impatient hand. She ought to consider herself lucky, she chided. That could have happened to her. And what would she have done with a baby? What would her father have thought then?

She sniffed. She was remembering how she had felt in those weeks before she'd known for certain that she wasn't pregnant. For a brief spell she had actually hoped she was expecting Matthew's baby. It would have been something of him to cherish. Someone who needed her love.

A bang, louder than the rest, startled her out of her reverie. And then the doorbell rang, echoing round the quiet house with loud insistence. Samantha looked at the clock. It was half-past nine. Who on earth would call so late in the evening? Her nerves tingled apprehensively. Who knew she was here alone?

Paul!

Her breath escaped in a rush, and she got up unwillingly from the couch. Only Paul knew the rest of the family was away on holiday. Only Paul was likely to call so late. And, although she had heard he was seeing someone else, she wouldn't put it past her father to have asked him to look in on her. Mr Maxwell still held out the hope that his daughter might change her mind. It didn't seem to occur to him that Paul's new girlfriend was unlikely to appreciate his interference.

It was dark in the hall, and Samantha was suddenly reluctant to turn on the light. What if it wasn't Paul? she fretted. How many times had women been warned about the dangers of opening their doors after dark? She could be in line to be the first victim of the Northfleet strangler! Murderers had to start somewhere, didn't they?

The doorbell didn't ring again, and she leaned uncertainly against the wall. Perhaps whoever it was had gone away. It could have been someone delivering circulars. But the letterbox didn't provide any clues.

She sighed, and straightened. This was ridiculous, she thought grimly. She wouldn't relax until she'd opened that door and made sure there was no one outside. It could be a thief, of course, checking to see if anyone was at home. At least if she opened the door she'd prove there was.

She unlocked the door without giving herself any more time to change her mind. Then, inching it open, she peered out. The wind swept into her face, bringing a scattering of leaves into the hallway. But, although the front gate was swinging back and forth, the caller seemed to have vanished.

And then she heard a groan from somewhere near the ground, and she let out a startled cry. A man was propped on the doorstep, his shoulders hunched, his body curled in on himself, as if he was in pain. Her initial reaction was to slam the door and call the police. But there was something about his appearance that was achingly familiar.

Dear God! Her throat went dry, and instead of slamming the door she squatted down on her haunches beside him. His head was lolling, and it was an easy matter to turn his face to the light. 'Matt!' she breathed, wondering with a sense of alarm if she was hallucinating. How could he be here, sitting on her doorstep? He didn't even know where she lived.

But it was him. Dark eyes, which seemed somehow glazed, lifted to her face. 'Sam,' he said, and she could have sworn he sounded relieved. 'Hell, Sam, isn't this the damnedest thing? I seem to have lost the use of my legs.'

Samantha stared at him helplessly. She couldn't believe he was here. It was like the answer to her dreams, and she wanted to take him in her arms. But once again common sense came to her rescue.

'Are—are you ill?' she asked, curling her nails into her palms, to prevent herself from touching him, and Matthew grimaced.

'No,' he replied. 'I don't think so.' He uttered a short laugh. 'Give me a hand up, will you? This is what comes of drinking Scotch on an empty stomach.'

Samantha blinked. 'You mean—you're drunk?' She scrambled to her feet, contempt for herself, and resentment at his habitual indifference to anyone's feelings but his own, contorting her face. The pathetic dreams she had had about him crumbled about her feet! She couldn't imagine why he was here, but it wouldn't do her any good.

'No, I'm not drunk,' Matthew muttered now, and, grabbing hold of the door frame, he hauled himself up. 'I guess I should have eaten something before I left the office.' He frowned, and pushed back his overlong hair with a weary hand. 'I can't remember when I last had any food.'

Samantha didn't know whether she believed him, but she took a step back and looked at him more thoroughly. He didn't look drunk, she conceded, seeing no evidence of that state in his tired eyes. He looked pale, and exhausted, and he had definitely lost weight. But now that he was on his feet he looked more sinned against than sinning.

It reminded her that she was hardly dressed for callers either. Her baggy dungarees, worn over an old sweater, and the woolly slippers on her feet, were hardly flattering. In addition to which, it was weeks since she had done anything but run a brush through her hair. In consequence, it now hung straight and unstyled, way past her shoulders.

'How—how did you get here?' she questioned, unable to bring herself to ask why he was here, and Matthew turned and gestured towards the road.

'In that,' he said, indicating an unremarkable black saloon parked at the kerb. 'And before you ask, I didn't take a drink until I passed your local. I guess I chose the wrong kind of Dutch courage.'

Samantha clutched the door. 'Dutch courage?' she echoed disbelievingly. 'Why would you need Dutch courage?'

'Why do you think?' retorted Matthew wearily, propping himself against the door. 'Can I come in? I need to talk to you.'

Samantha didn't move. 'How—how did you know where I lived?'

Matthew sighed. 'I looked you up in the phone book.'

'Our number's not in the phone book.'

'Oh, for Pete's sake!' Matthew's red-rimmed eyes bored into hers. 'OK. I had someone find out, right? Now—can I come in? Or do I have to ask your father?'

Samantha licked her lips. 'My father's not here.'

Matthew's eyes flickered. 'But this is his house,' he probed warily, and she nodded. 'So,' he seemed to breathe a little more easily after that, 'let's find somewhere less public to talk.'

Samantha swallowed. 'What about?'

Matthew sighed again. 'You and me.'

'You and me?' Samantha stepped back almost involuntarily, and he took advantage of her momentary lapse to step inside. Supporting himself, with his back against the coat-rack, he closed the door. Then, as if he couldn't help himself, he closed his eyes, groping for a handhold to prevent another collapse.

'I'm sorry,' he muttered, opening his eyes again, and in spite of her misgivings Samantha found herself offering him her shoulder to lean on. With some difficulty, she managed to get him along the hall and into the sitting-room, then watched with anxious eyes as he lowered himself on to the sofa.

He looked much worse in the brighter light of the sitting-room. His eyes were haggard, and his face was drained of all colour. He lay back against the cushions as if it was days since he had had any rest. And, although she told herself it was nothing to do with her, she couldn't prevent the wave of compassion that swept over her.

'Are your parents out?' he asked, making an evident effort to hide his weakness, and Samantha decided that there was no point in telling lies.

'They're not here,' she said. 'They're on holiday in Tenerife. They only left this morning.'

Matthew hauled himself upright. 'For how long? I mean—how long have they gone for?'

Samantha hesitated, and then mentally berated herself. What could he do? He was practically an invalid.

'Two weeks,' she answered now, hovering by the door. 'Um—do you want a sandwich or something? If you haven't eaten since lunchtime——'

'I haven't eaten since God knows when,' retorted Matthew harshly, pushing himself to the edge of the sofa, almost as if he intended getting up again. 'Sam——' He paused. 'Sam, are you still going to marry Webster? I have to know. I have to know where I stand. I don't know how much more of this I can take.'

Samantha quivered. 'How—how much more of what?'

'This!' He looked up at her impatiently, and then forced himself into a standing position. 'God, Sam, answer the question! Are you still engaged to Webster or not?'

She came forward then, her concern for his welfare outweighing her doubts about him being there. 'Sit down,' she said, putting her hands on his forearms. 'Sit down before you fall down! Look—I'll get you a sandwich, then we can talk——'

'Like hell!' he muttered savagely, and when she tried to urge him back on to the sofa he used her strength against her. He sank down but he took her with him, tumbling her on to his lap, and capturing her face in his hand. 'Tell me,' he demanded, and his eyes glittered with a sense of purpose she wouldn't have believed he possessed. 'You know that I'm in love with you. Can't you at least put me out of my misery?'

Samantha gazed at him. His warm breath, only slightly flavoured with whisky, was fanning her temple, and he smelt of soap, and cigarette smoke, and the sharp autumn air. It was months since she'd seen him, yet she felt she knew every pore of his features, and her hands itched to smooth the long unruly hair back from his forehead.

'No,' she said at last, realising there was nowhere to run any more. 'I—broke my engagement to Paul months ago. Right—right after that night I spent on the island.'

'You didn't!' Matthew grasped her face between hands that even she could feel were trembling. 'Sam, do you mean to tell me you weren't engaged to Webster that day I came to the café?'

She nodded.

He shook his head. 'But why? Did——' He broke off, and then continued doggedly, 'Was I responsible? Oh, God, what I'm trying to say is, did I destroy your life?'

Samantha clutched the lapels of his jacket, the need to get nearer to him overwhelming any lingering doubts. 'Only—only when you went away,' she got out huskily, gazing up at him with tear-wet eyes, and a dawning comprehension filled his gaze.

'Why—why didn't you tell me?' he demanded, smoothing back her hair with agitated fingers. 'Oh, God, Sam, I thought that was what you wanted.'

'I—I was afraid,' she admitted, putting up her hands now and cupping his face. 'I loved you, and I was afraid.' There was no point in denying it any longer. He could have his revenge, if he wanted. She wouldn't stop him. So long as they were together, her life would have some meaning again.

'Oh, Sam!'

Matthew's groan was uttered against her mouth, and his arms slid convulsively around her. With a tenderness he had never shown before, he wrapped her in his protection, cradling her against him as if he'd never let her go.

It was some minutes before they spoke again, minutes of warmth, and passion, and heart-stopping sweetness. Matthew couldn't seem to get enough of her, and kisses that had begun so gently soon became an urgent duel of tongues.

But at last he dragged himself away, and rested his forehead against hers. 'You're not going to send me away again, are you?' he demanded huskily. 'I mean, I know I've made mistakes, but I think I've got a chance now to put things right.'

Samantha was shaking, but she managed to move her head from side to side. She realised it wouldn't be easy convincing her parents that what she was doing was right. But she had proved she couldn't live without Matthew, so whatever happened she would have to live with him.

'OK,' he said, and she could tell he was near the end of his strength. 'We'll get married, as soon as I can get a licence.'

'Married?'

The astonishment in her voice caused him to gaze at her a little anxiously, but then her weight, and his own weakness, caused him to slump sideways on to the sofa.

'Yes, married,' he said, his arms falling away from her. 'Sam, don't argue, *please*! Not till I've had some sleep.'

It was the sound of the shower that alerted her to the fact that Matthew was awake. She hadn't heard him come upstairs, but then the wind had been buffeting the house all night, and she had grown used to hearing unusual creaks and groans.

She hadn't slept much. Her mind had been too active. Besides, just the thought that Matthew was asleep on the sofa downstairs was enough to keep her adrenalin running. She kept having to pinch herself to make sure it wasn't just a dream. But when she'd tiptoed downstairs in the early hours, and draped a blanket over him, his pale, well-loved features were incredibly real.

She glanced at the clock. It was just after six, which was why it was still fairly dark outside. She wondered if Matthew had seen the sandwich and the flask of coffee she had left for him. Well, at least he had had the strength to climb the stairs, she thought. And there was something very reassuring in listening to him taking a shower.

She had tried not to think about what he had said before exhaustion conquered him. He had asked her to marry him, and she should have been overjoyed. But his proposal reminded her of who he was, and what was expected of him. And even though she loved him she doubted it would be enough.

The landing creaked outside her door, and for a moment she stopped breathing. But when the door remained unopened she slid out of bed, and went to see what he was doing.

He was just coming out of her parents' room. He was naked, except for the towel he had slung about his waist, and his wet hair clung damply to his neck. 'What are you doing?' she asked in an undertone, and then realised how unnecessary it was for her to whisper. But there was something delightfully wicked about their being here alone together, in her parents' house, and when he turned to face her her knees felt distinctly weak.

'I was looking for you,' he said simply, and she could see in the light that streamed out of the bathroom how much less exhausted he looked. He crossed the landing, and gave her modest lawn nightdress an appraising look. 'Let's go to bed,' he added thickly. 'It's still the middle of the night.'

Hours later, Samantha awakened to find Matthew was already awake, watching her. In spite of all the intimacies they had shared she was still incapable of meeting his lazy gaze without blushing, and he deliberately turned the covers back so that he could kiss one creamy breast.

'I love you,' he breathed, his tongue dampening the taut nipple. 'Did I tell you that already?'

'Sev-several times,' she said unsteadily, her hand closing round his nape and holding him against her. 'Oh, Matt—I'm glad you came last night.'

'Hmm, so am I,' he agreed, moving so that she could feel his arousal against her. 'So—when are you going to make an honest man of me?'

'Oh, Matt!' She shifted then, not turning away from him exactly, but putting an inch of the narrow mattress between them. 'You—you don't *have* to marry me. I'm not making any conditions. Not this time.'

'I am.' Matthew followed her, only this time he imprisoned her beneath the muscled strength of his body. 'Do you think I'm going to take a chance on you walking out on me again? Oh, no. You're going to be Mrs Matthew Putnam. I want everyone to know exactly who you are.'

Samantha caught her lower lip between her teeth. 'Including your family.'

'*Especially* my family,' agreed Matthew forcefully. He bent to bestow a lingering kiss at the corner of her mouth.

'So your children know who their father is?' suggested Samantha softly, and Matthew groaned.

'You know,' he said, 'it did cross my mind that I might have made you pregnant.' His thumb brushed over her lips. 'You weren't on the Pill, were you?' And at her denial, 'Believe it or not, I actually hoped I had. I'd have done anything to get you back.'

Samantha frowned. 'But you didn't come back.'

'No.' Matthew stroked her shoulder. 'Not after I'd made sure you were still seeing Webster. The only thing I didn't know was that you hadn't married him. But—thanks to my grandfather—I eventually got up the courage to find out.'

'What do you mean? How did you know I was still seeing Paul?'

Matthew's cheeks gained a little colour. 'How do you think?'

'You had me followed?' Samantha gasped.

'Well——' He was unrepentant. 'At first I couldn't believe you'd go through with your engagement. But—when the reports came in——'

'Paul wouldn't take no for an answer. I—I told him about you——'

'Did you?' Matthew's mouth quirked.

'—but he still kept coming to the house.' She paused. 'Not any longer, though. He's got another girlfriend now.'

'Has he?' Matthew hesitated. 'And how do you feel about that?'

'Pleased. Relieved.' Samantha shifted a little restlessly beneath him. 'Matt, I can't breathe.'

'Good,' he said, somewhat smugly, but he moved so that his thigh was resting between hers. 'Ah, God! Is that the time? I have an appointment for lunch at half-past twelve.'

Samantha looked up at him. 'Are you going?' she asked, a little anxiously, and his smile gave his gaunt features a disturbing attraction.

'Not without you,' he told her gently. 'It's very convenient, actually. I'm having lunch with my mother at the Savoy.'

'Oh!'

Samantha's mouth drew in, and Matthew laughed softly at her obvious dismay. 'It's time she met the future Mrs Putnam,' he said firmly. 'Don't worry. She knows when she's beaten.'

'What do you mean?'

'I mean my grandfather told her yesterday, in no uncertain terms, that she had ruined my life. He said if she hadn't interfered, and sent you back to England, we would probably have been married by now.'

Samantha gasped. 'I don't believe you.'

'It's true.' Matthew grinned. 'Would I lie?'

'You have done, on occasion,' she told him severely, and he shrugged.

'Only to get what I wanted,' he replied irrepressibly. 'And I've wanted you since the first moment I saw you.'

'But——' Samantha made one last attempt to be serious. 'I don't know whether I want to be like your mother. Being—being rich doesn't seem to have made her happy, does it?'

'I don't want you to be like my mother either,' retorted Matthew fervently. 'Which is why I've persuaded my grandfather to make her the nominal head of the Apollonius Corporation when he retires. You and I are going to live in London, and I'm going to go on running J.P. Software. By the time Caroline gets tired of giving orders, you and I will be putting our grandchildren to bed.' He smiled. 'Now—will you marry me?'

And as Samantha agreed she knew that heaven was within her grasp...

HARLEQUIN®

PRESENTS® plus

Meet Lewis Marsh, the man who walked out of Lacey's life twenty years ago. Now he's back, but is time really a cure for love?

And then there's widower Jim Proctor, whose young daughter, Maude, needs a mother. Lucy needs a job, but does she really need a husband?

These are just some of the passionate men and women you'll discover each month in Harlequin Presents Plus—two longer and dramatic new romances by some of the best-loved authors writing for Harlequin Presents. Share their exciting stories—their heartaches and triumphs—as each falls in love.

Don't miss
A CURE FOR LOVE by Penny Jordan,
Harlequin Presents Plus #1575
and
THE WIDOW'S MITE by Emma Goldrick,
Harlequin Presents Plus #1576

Harlequin Presents Plus
The best has just gotten better!

Available in August wherever Harlequin books are sold.

Relive the romance...
Harlequin and Silhouette
are proud to present

by Request

A program of collections of three complete novels by the most requested authors with the most requested themes. Be sure to look for one volume each month with three complete novels by top name authors.

In June: **NINE MONTHS** Penny Jordan
Stella Cameron
Janice Kaiser

Three women pregnant and alone. But a lot can happen in nine months!

In July: **DADDY'S HOME** Kristin James
Naomi Horton
Mary Lynn Baxter

Daddy's Home... and his presence is long overdue!

In August: **FORGOTTEN PAST** Barbara Kaye
Pamela Browning
Nancy Martin

Do you dare to create a future if you've forgotten the past?

Available at your favorite retail outlet.

WHEN STOLEN MOMENTS
ARE ALL YOU HAVE...

The sun is hot and you've got a few minutes
to catch some rays....

And what better way to spend the time than with
SUMMER MADNESS—our summer promotion that features
six new individual short contemporary stories.

SIZZLE	Jennifer Crusie
ANNIVERSARY WALTZ	Anne Marie Duquette
MAGGIE AND HER COLONEL	Merline Lovelace
PRAIRIE SUMMER	Alina Roberts
THE SUGAR CUP	Annie Sims
LOVE ME NOT	Barbara Stewart

Each story is a complete romance that's just the perfect length
for the busy woman of the nineties... but still providing the
perfect blend of adventure, sensuality and, of course, romance!

Look for the special displays in July and share some of the
Summer Madness!

HSM-1

HARLEQUIN PRESENTS®

A Year
DOWN UNDER

In 1993, Harlequin Presents celebrates the land down under. In August let us take you to Auckland and Northland, New Zealand, in THE STONE PRINCESS by Robyn Donald, Harlequin Presents #1577.

They'd parted eight years ago, but Petra still feels something for Caine Fleming. Now the handsome New Zealander wants to reconcile, but Petra isn't convinced of his true feelings for her. She does know that she wants— that she *needs*—any reconciliation to be more than a marriage of convenience. Petra wants Caine body and soul.

Share the adventure—and the romance—of
A Year Down Under!

Available this month in
A Year Down Under

NO RISKS, NO PRIZES
by Emma Darcy
Harlequin Presents #1570
Available wherever Harlequin books are sold.